Lauren saw Warwick standing by the car

Mandy's arm tightened convulsively about her and she cried, "Mummy!"

Lauren watched Warwick's eyes travel from her to Mandy. For one moment they rested on her hair. Then they returned again, and his face slowly whitened with shock. She had never seen a man go pale before — even his lips were drained of color — and she wondered dispassionately if men ever felt faint in the same way women did.

She stood quite still, one hand on Mandy's shoulder, reassuring and protective. Then with startling suddenness Warwick turned and got into the car. All Mandy could say over and over, was, "Don't let him come back, Mummy!"

"He won't, darling," Lauren assured her. He would never come back now.

WELCOME
TO THE WONDERFUL WORLD
OF *Harlequin Romances*

Interesting, informative and entertaining,
each Harlequin Romance portrays an appealing
and original love story. With a varied array
of settings, we may lure you on an African safari,
to a quaint Welsh village, or an exotic Riviera
location—anywhere and everywhere that adventurous
men and women fall in love.

As publishers of Harlequin Romances, we're
extremely proud of our books. Since 1949,
Harlequin Enterprises has built its publishing
reputation on the solid base of quality and
originality. Our stories are the most popular
paperback romances sold in North America; every
month, six new titles are released and sold at
nearly every book-selling store in Canada and the
United States.

For a list of all titles currently available,
send your name and address to:

HARLEQUIN READER SERVICE,
(In the U.S.) P.O. Box 52040, Phoenix, AZ 85072-2040
(In Canada) P.O. Box 2800, Postal Station A
5170 Yonge Street, Willowdale, Ont.   M2N 6J3

We sincerely hope you enjoy reading
this Harlequin Romance.

Yours truly,

THE PUBLISHERS
Harlequin Romances

Echo
of Betrayal

Valerie Marsh

Harlequin Books

TORONTO • NEW YORK • LONDON
AMSTERDAM • PARIS • SYDNEY • HAMBURG
STOCKHOLM • ATHENS • TOKYO • MILAN

Original hardcover edition published in 1984
by Mills & Boon Limited

ISBN 0-373-02676-5

Harlequin Romance first edition February 1985

Printed in U.S.A.

CHAPTER ONE

LAUREN glanced at her watch again and then at the door to the inner office, the muscles of her stomach tightening nervously. There were two letters which *must* be answered in tonight's post, and if he didn't come out of there soon . . .

She could hear the murmur of voices through the closed door, Warwick Sinclair's deep tones and the Frenchman's lighter ones, the accent discernible even though she couldn't distinguish the words. They were both laughing now, and in exasperation she pulled the letters towards her. She could perfectly well reply to them herself, but dared she? And wouldn't Mr Warwick Sinclair want a phrase altered here and there out of sheer bloodymindedness if she did?

The advancing minute hand of her watch decided her. Rolling the paper into the typewriter, she swiftly headed it up and paused for a moment to compose the wording in Warwick's distinctive style. Reading them through afterwards, Lauren thought she had achieved a fair imitation, though it was doubtful if that was any guarantee of satisfaction.

Her eyes on the time again, she cleared off her desk and was putting the cover on her typewriter when the intercom buzzed. Depressing the switch, she said, 'Yes, Mr Sinclair?' and he told her abruptly, 'Have the car sent round to the front for Monsieur Rouillière. He'll be leaving shortly.'

'Thank heavens for that!' Lauren thought from the heart, briskly conveying the message. If they didn't linger over their farewells she might still catch her

connecting bus and there surely couldn't be much more
for them to say to one another. The meeting had begun
in the morning, continued through an extended and no
doubt expensive lunch, and gone on to occupy the last
two hours in the inner office. Warwick had ordered no
interruptions or phone calls, and she had been stalling
one of his current girl-friends all day.

The extension rang and she snatched it up, to hear
the switchboard girl say wearily, 'Hasn't he got a home
to go to? Some of us haven't spent half the day lunching
and boozing, and we have the relaxing luxury of a
journey by public transport ahead of us. Can't you root
him out of there, or at least ask him if I can put the
phones through?'

Lauren held the receiver away from her ear and
regarded it with incredulity for a moment, then
returned tartly, 'You're joking, I trust!' Though Meg
was only echoing her own thoughts, perversely she
found herself defending Warwick. 'He's got a very
important customer with him. I think this is a big deal
if it comes off.'

Meg sighed. 'Could you tell that to his darling Petra?
I've got her breathing hurt feelings and disbelief down
the line at me again.'

'Put her through,' Lauren said briefly.

Petra came on, her well-bred voice tremulous with
tears, and Lauren said, 'I'm sorry, but he's still in
there.'

'If Rick refuses to speak to me I would rather you
told me,' Petra stated in quivering tones.

'He refuses to speak to anyone, including me,'
Lauren informed her. 'And if he doesn't come out soon
he can run his letters through the franking machine
himself and have the rare pleasure of posting them with
his own fair hands.'

Petra cheered up immediately. Giggling, she asked,

'Would he know how to? Use a franking machine, I mean.'

'Oh, I should think it would be just about within his capabilities,' Lauren said drily, vaguely surprised to find that the gorgeous but empty-headed Petra knew what it was. She wondered if Warwick ever actually talked to her; there must surely be some portion of their time together that wasn't spent in bed.

As though she had picked up the surprise, Petra said, 'I used to help Daddy in his office sometimes when his secretary was away, though I couldn't do shorthand or anything like that, of course.'

Daddy must have been desperate, Lauren reflected. Aloud, she said, 'You can have my job any time.'

'Oh, I don't think I should like working for Rick,' Petra said seriously. 'He can be terribly overpowering, I know.'

Overpowering? Lauren thought as she replaced the receiver. Was that all? She could add a few stronger descriptions herself, and so no doubt would Petra in the fullness of time. Fidelity was not Warwick's most noticeable characteristic, and apparently she had yet to discover that he was also escorting the no less glamorous but rather more intelligent Vivian. Lauren usually got his calls for him in the office, and on more than one occasion she had almost given in to the appalling temptation to dial the wrong number for the sheer pleasure of listening to him try to get out of the furore it would cause.

She admitted to herself that she was never likely to actually do it—she was far too afraid of him, but it made an agreeable daydream.

Warwick's door opened suddenly, startling her, and she saw him gesturing the Frenchman through. Monsieur Rouillière, small and dark and at least fifty, paused by her desk to exclaim, 'Ah, what hair! Such a

glorious colour!' and, amused, she smiled at him, trying
to ignore the icy glare Warwick directed at her. The two
men disappeared into the corridor, the Frenchman
protesting that there was no need to accompany him.
Lauren heard the whine as the lift descended, then
Warwick was back.

He leaned on the doorpost for a moment and she
found herself intimidated as always by his sheer size.
His brows were drawn together so that they formed a
single line over his strong nose and eyes so dark they
were almost black. Together with his black hair they
gave him a foreign look, so that his ultra-English name
always came as something of a shock. Lauren had
frequently seen people give a double-take when they
heard it for the first time.

He stared at her now in cold temper, then strode
across to her desk, demanding, 'Why didn't you go the
whole hog and put your coat on and switch the lights
off while you were at it?'

It took Lauren a moment to realise that her offence
had been to put the cover on her typewriter, but before
she could speak he went on bitingly, 'The French
already think we're a nation of strike-happy clock-
watchers! Do you *have* to confirm their opinion? This is
a damned important deal, and if it comes off it will pay
yours and everyone's else's wages for the next twelve
months! Half an hour more of your time wouldn't kill
you just this once!'

Lauren felt her stomach contract again, but she said
steadily, 'Mr Sinclair, I made it plain when you offered
me this job that I couldn't ever work over except . . .'

'I know!' he interrupted savagely. 'Except on
Tuesdays and Thursdays by prior arrangement! But you
know how the workload comes in fits and starts. How
the hell do I know in advance when I'm going to need
you?'

She lowered her eyes again. 'Then you shouldn't have taken me on. I was quite frank with you.'

'You were,' he allowed curtly. 'The mistake was mine. I hadn't fully realised you would apply the overtime ban quite so rigidly. Is there a typist left in the building? I need these first thing in the morning!'

He flung a batch of scrawled notes down on her desk, and Lauren stared at them helplessly. He knew perfectly well that everyone in the typing pool would have left by now. The sole object of his question was to make her feel worse. She said at last, 'I've got a typewriter at home. It's a bit old and it isn't electric, but if they aren't things that have to be sent out . . .' Her voice trailed away, then she saw that Warwick's expression had relaxed slightly, and dared to add, 'I knew you might be tied up a long time, so I answered the two urgent letters myself.' She pushed the folder towards him, watching him apprehensively. 'I hope they're all right.'

While he was reading them she risked another quick glance at her watch, and regretted it when she looked up to find his eyes fixed on her. His expression hardened again.

'What the hell *is* so vital that you can never stay a second over? And don't tell me you've got an invalid mother, because I happen to know she died about a year ago!'

In quick alarm she asked, 'How did you know that?'

'I sent down for you to do some work for me and you were away. Personnel told me.' His acute gaze rested on her for a moment, then he scanned through the letters again. 'These will do. Lend me your pen.'

Lauren's lips tightened as she handed it over. Occasionally, just occasionally, he might give her a little deserved credit. She folded the letters swiftly and stuck down the envelopes, using a couple of stamps out of the reserve in her drawer. 'I'll drop them in at the post office on my way home.'

He nodded absently, his attention on the pages of notes. 'I'd better go through these with you first if you're going to type them. You may not be able to read Rouillière's writing in some of the technical terms.' Catching her expression, he added, 'Oh, don't panic! It shouldn't take more than ten minutes, and I'll run you home afterwards.'

'No!'

The single word broke from her with more force than she intended, and his glance sharpened and became intent. 'Why not?'

Lamely, she said, 'Well, it must be out of your way.'

'I realised that when I made the offer.' His narrowed eyes measured her. 'As you must have known.' He paused, still watching her, then impatient again, went on, 'Now if you're so desperate to get away, go through these and tell me anything you can't read or understand. I shall want them grouped under separate headings, but I'll write those in as we go along.'

He leaned his knuckles on the polished surface of the desk as he spoke, and before she could prevent herself Lauren had flinched away. He noticed, of course, as he always did, and met her eyes, his temper barely held in check. 'Miss Peters, fifty per cent of the population is made up of the male of the species. Eventually you are going to have to accept that fact and come to terms with it!'

'Aren't you forgetting I'm engaged?' Lauren returned defiantly.

'No, though it never ceases to astound me.' He stood back ostentatiously. 'And you might have told me you were contemplating it when I set you on.'

'I didn't know myself at the time. And it doesn't make any difference.'

'Engaged women tend to get married and married ones tend to leave. I don't like a constant turnover.'

His tone carried the implication that it was the only reason she was still working for him. And perhaps not for much longer, if he went on like this, Lauren thought resentfully. Suddenly weary, she said, 'Mr Sinclair, I'm twenty-four, so it can't have been entirely unexpected. I'm not planning to get married for a long time, and when I do I shall carry on working, so you needn't have any worries on that score.'

He regarded her cynically. 'It can't have escaped your notice that married women frequently get pregnant, whether they intend to or not. If the rumours about a certain careless young woman in the typing pool are true it can even happen without benefit of matrimony.'

Her face flamed scarlet and he gave a sigh of resignation. 'The word pregnant is common usage. It doesn't cause raised eyebrows in even the most polite circles.' He watched the tide of colour fade from her face and picked up the notes impatiently. 'Now, for God's sake let's go through these. I want to get away as well, remarkable though that may seem.'

Lauren bent over the sheets, then suddenly remembering, said, 'Oh, Miss Scott rang you several times. I told her you couldn't be disturbed.'

'Go on telling her that,' he said shortly.

She gave him a level look, and with a burst of recklessness said, 'I'm prepared to cover for you when it's business, Mr Sinclair—it's my job and I'm paid for it, but I should be grateful if you would do your own dirty work where your private life is concerned.'

There was a long silence and she felt a prickle of fright at what she had done, then, soft-voiced, he said, 'Miss Peters, you are a very capable and efficient secretary, I grant you, but you aren't unique in that, and it wouldn't be impossible to find another with all your attributes.' He left a pause, then finished even more gently, 'Don't tempt me.'

She paled under his menacing stare and muttered, 'I'm sorry.'

Taking the notes from him with hands that trembled slightly, she forced herself to concentrate on the Frenchman's untidy writing, following the lines with her pen and pausing where she was unsure of a word for Warwick to clarify it. He wrote in the headings and numbered the paragraphs where he wanted them in a different order, and when it was completed she slipped them into a folder and stood up.

'Will you want copies?'

'At least twenty, so you'll have to photo-copy them. Do them first thing when you come in. Have you got a coat?'

Lauren shook her head and started towards the door. 'There's no need for you to run me home. It won't take me so long now the rush hour's over.'

'Miss Peters?'

Unwillingly she halted and half turned towards him. His voice deliberate, he asked, 'Why are you so anxious to avoid me taking you home?'

Her heart was pounding so hard it seemed he must hear it, but she managed to say indifferently, 'I'm not in the least anxious. It just seems a waste of your time.'

'Then I'll be the judge of that. Meet me outside the front doors. I'll tell the security guard we're on our way down.'

She shrugged and continued on her way, hurrying in spite of herself once she was in the corridor, even though she recognised that it couldn't make any difference to the time she got home. She still had to wait for Warwick to bring the car up from the underground garage, so time saved now would only be wasted outside until he came.

She forced her feet to slow, trying to control the waves of apprehension rolling over her. Her previous anxiety at being late was nothing compared with her fear of what Warwick could discover at the end of the journey. She wondered if she could persuade him to drop her at the end of the road, and searching her mind for some credible excuse, she hardly registered the security guard's words as he unlocked the doors for her. Answering him almost at random, she stepped from behind the tinted glass to the brilliant sunshine outside.

As she waited on the pavement one of her buses came down the street towards her, and she had taken half a dozen steps before reason reasserted itself. She had pushed Warwick far enough in his present mood. If he found she had gone it really would be the end of her job and she might never get another with the same pay. It had been a moment of madness when she told him to do his own dirty work, and she went cold when she thought of it now. She simply couldn't risk it.

She retraced her steps and was standing by the kerb when the familiar metallic grey Porsche drew up beside her. Warwick must have grown particularly fond of this one to keep it so long. Normally he changed his cars nearly as often as his women, and the whole building was almost immediately aware when he had a new edition of either. The girl in Reception reported the cars, and there were few secrets from a telephonist, especially as Warwick made no attempt to hide them. Lauren wondered if he knew that his personal calls were a popular topic of conversation at lunch times, though he obviously wouldn't care. Probably he was proud of his philandering image.

She became aware that he had pushed the car door open and was saying impatiently, 'I'm on double yellows!' and getting in quickly, she balanced her bag and folder on her knee. Uncomfortable because of the

enforced proximity in the car, she leaned away from
him so there was no possibility of accidental contact.
She didn't offer her address. He probably knew it, and
if he didn't he could ask.

Watching her, he said gently, 'Safety-belt, Miss
Peters.'

'Oh, yes.'

For some reason flustered, she remained nervously
silent as he negotiated the traffic. She was used to
encountering it from the reassuring bulk of a London
bus and she felt vulnerable in the low car. Her
nervousness apparently communicated itself to
Warwick, and he looked across at her with a mixture of
amusement and irritation.

'Relax. I'm accounted a reasonably competent
driver.'

Lauren wondered what he would say if he knew she
travelled in cars so rarely she was totally unable to
judge anyone's driving ability. In this day and age it
would be hard to believe, but she could count on one
hand the number of times she had been in one in the
last couple of years. They were alien and unfamiliar,
and when Warwick said, 'Pull your sun visor down,' she
only stared at him uncomprehendingly.

They had turned directly into the lowering sun's rays,
and blinded by the glare, she didn't see the movement
of his arm as he reached over to pull the visor down.
Shielded, her vision adjusted and she turned away
quickly from the sight of his bare forearm in front of
her. She had never seen him without his jacket, but he
had obviously discarded it before getting into the car
and his shirtsleeves were rolled up above his elbows.

She had worked for him for ten months now and he
had long been aware of her abhorrence of physical
contact of any kind. At times he used the knowledge to
plague her, deliberately moving close enough to make

her tense, but not near enough for her to raise any reasonable objection. However much she tried she could not control that involuntary stiffening of her muscles, and even when Warwick had wantonly provoked it himself she knew that it still annoyed him.

From the tightening of his jaw she knew he had seen it now, but his tone was expressionless when he said, 'Describe your fiancé for me.'

She looked at him warily. He seldom asked questions without a definite motive. 'Why?'

'Curiosity.' He shrugged. 'Not laudable perhaps, but neither is it a crime.'

She could tell him to mind his own business, but it wasn't a good idea to antagonise him again, so she said, 'About five feet eleven, brown hair, grey eyes and twenty-eight.'

'Succinct,' Warwick commented. 'What does he do for a living?'

'He's in the Navy.'

'What rank?'

Oh, God, what would Trevor be now? His mother had mentioned it in one of her letters, but she couldn't remember. Repressively she returned, 'Nothing very important.'

'Where is he now? Here in London?'

'No, he's doing six months at sea. He has four to go.' That much was accurate at least.

'That follows.'

There was derision in his voice, and Lauren glanced at him sharply. 'What do you mean?'

He shot her a swift glance, taking his eyes from the road only fleetingly. 'A husband in the Navy. For six months at a time you'll be able to pretend you're single again.'

He had completely silenced her and knew it. Whatever she said now would be bound to lead down even more embarrassing avenues. On occasions he seemed to delight in making her feel small, and she wondered again why he had kept her on after her trial period was up. She was extremely efficient, but as he so charmingly pointed out, efficient secretaries were ten a penny, and he could easily find one willing to share his bed as well as taking his dictation.

Stealing a glance at his uncompromising profile, she supposed most women would eventually give in to his lure if he set his mind to it. He was a handsome man by any standards, and in addition he possessed that physical aura which had nothing to do with looks and was defined by the senses rather than the brain. Even Meg, who professed to hate him, would turn to watch when he walked through her office. The girls in the typing pool frankly swooned, but then it was rare for them to have anything to do with him. Lauren never had herself when she was down there, except for two days when his secretary was ill and he had sent down for someone to do the routine typing. Her present job had come six months later.

She still didn't know whether her elevation had been a good or a bad thing. The huge increase in salary was welcome, but working for Warwick was a strain. To be under stress seven hours a day, five days a week, was as bad in its way as worrying over money.

A small sigh escaped her, then her blank gaze focussed and she realised she was nearly home. In jolting alarm she said quickly, 'You can drop me here. It will save you turning round and it's only a little way along.'

He had been driving slowly, scanning the numbers, but he glanced at her swiftly and she read speculation in his eyes. 'Number forty-seven,' he said evenly. 'It's at the other end. It must be half a mile.'

Oh, damn the man! she thought frantically. She had

betrayed herself when she let him see she didn't want him to run her home, and now he wanted to know why. In her agitation she let the folder slide from her knees and the pages scattered about her feet. She tried to move too quickly when she bent to pick them up and the safety-belt locked, holding her rigidly in her seat.

Pulling in smoothly outside the Victorian terraced house where she lived, Warwick pushed the belt back to free the mechanism, then reached down to release the clip. He had touched her deliberately, she knew, his hand resting against her longer than was necessary, but for once she was too distraught to care.

Jerkily, she said, 'I must go in quickly. Thank you for bringing me home.'

She was out of the car and almost running when he called, 'Miss Peters!'

Her eyes fixed in panic on the figure behind the net curtains at the downstairs window, Lauren forced herself to stop and turn back.

Warwick was standing by the car, his expression half exasperated, half amused as he held the folder out to her, the letters in his other hand. She waited for some sarcastic comment, but searching her face he registered her agitation and the words were checked. For a moment his gaze went beyond her as though the shabby frontage and grimed brickwork might give some clue to her overwrought state, then he seemed to take pity on her. Thrusting the folder into her outstretched hand, he merely said, 'Here! Your typewriter isn't much use without these!'

CHAPTER TWO

As she watched the rear of the car disappear round the bend, the sick feeling in Lauren's stomach gradually subsided. She turned back to the door, but before she could find her key it opened, a small figure poised on tiptoe to reach the lock.

'Hello, Sarah,' Lauren said warmly. 'How long have you been able to do that?'

'Just this minute. I tried this morning and I couldn't, but now I can.' Solemnly, Sarah added, 'You're late, Auntie Lauren.'

Lauren pulled a wry face as she followed her into the hall. 'I know, darling. Was Mummy worried?'

'She told me to watch for you by the window. Mandy waited for you at first, but you were so long coming she got tired.'

'Where is she now?' Lauren enquired.

'Playing in the garden, I think,' Sarah said vaguely. 'Shall I go and see?'

When Lauren nodded she went to the back door and called, 'Your Mummy's come home!' and a few seconds later Mandy erupted, squealing, through the door.

Lauren caught her up in her arms. 'Hello, darling. Let's go and find Auntie Ann.'

'I'm here,' said Ann, coming out of the kitchen. 'It's all right, I heard you come in, though I admit I was getting a bit restless. What happened?'

'Near disaster,' Lauren told her, grimacing. 'My insides still haven't properly settled. My lovable boss was closeted with someone in his office, so I couldn't leave, then he insisted on running me home. I was in

total terror in case Mandy was in the window as usual.'
Lightly tugging her daughter's long rope of red hair, she
shuddered. 'One glimpse of this ...! God, I was
petrified!'

'Oh, for goodness' sake, tell the man,' Ann advised.
'Save the wear on your nerves!'

She shrugged at Lauren's warning look, and Mandy
asked, 'What does petri ... petri ... what does that
word mean?'

'That you've got hair the same colour as your
mother's,' Ann said drily.

Mandy chewed her bottom lip in puzzlement and
Lauren smiled then glanced up at Ann. 'Did you know
Sarah can reach the lock on the front door now?'

Ann groaned. 'I'll worry about it when I get home. I
haven't got time at the moment.' She snatched up her
coat from behind the door. 'Goodbye, Mandy—
goodbye, Sarah. Be good for Auntie Lauren.'

'I always am, aren't I?' Sarah appealed to Lauren.

'Most of the time,' Lauren agreed.

She went into the front room and eased off her shoes,
spreading her toes in relief. Mandy switched the
television on and Lauren watched in amusement as the
two children sat enthralled by an advertisement for fish
fingers.

'We have those,' said Sarah, apparently pleased to
find their choice endorsed. She climbed on to the settee
and wormed her way under Lauren's arm. 'Why do you
go to work in the daytime and Mummy in the night-
time?'

'So that Mummy could look after you if you were
poorly and couldn't go to school, and she can be here
to give you your tea. Then Mummy goes to work in the
evening while I'm here to look after you.'

'Why does Mummy have to go to work?'

'To earn the money to buy your fish fingers.'

'Why?'

'Because our daddies went away, of course,' Mandy said matter-of-factly. 'Everybody knows that.' Her faintly patronising air deserting her, she turned to Lauren. 'Melissa in our class says she's got two daddies. How can anyone have two?' With a hint of tears she added, 'It's not fair when we haven't got one at all!'

Lauren pulled a rueful face, but before she could phrase her reply, Mandy was distracted. Twisting round, she said, 'Why have you got that pretty ring on instead of the yellow one?'

'Damn Warwick Sinclair!' Lauren thought. This was his fault as well. Normally she changed them over before she got home, but in the heat of the moment she had forgotten she was still wearing the engagement ring.

She held her hand out. 'It is pretty, isn't it? I just thought I would wear it today, that's all. Pass my bag to me, darling, and I'll change them back now.'

'I like that one better,' Sarah remarked. 'It sparkles. Why are you changing them back?'

'Because married ladies always wear one of those yellow ones, silly,' Mandy told her.

'Don't call Sarah silly,' Lauren reprimanded automatically. 'Remember you're a year older than she is.' She eased herself gently free of the two pairs of entwining arms. 'I've got to go and do some typing in the kitchen. Watch the television quietly and don't quarrel.'

Picking up her bag and folder, she went out, but after she had set the typewriter up on the table she sat for a long time thinking. Had she been wrong to hide from Mandy the fact that she was illegitimate? Perhaps it would have been better to tell her while she was still so young that it could have no real meaning for her. The trouble was that other children could be so terrifyingly cruel.

Lauren remembered her own young days at school when for a time she had been the only child in the class with divorced parents. The others had been merciless when they discovered she minded. She could still recall the feeling they had managed to give her of being a second class citizen.

Absently she began to put Monsieur Rouillière's notes back in order as she pondered. She didn't know whether she was right or wrong. The whole climate had changed so much from when she was young herself, and Mandy wasn't the desperately shy, introverted child that her own mother had made of her. Looking back, she knew her mother had always disliked her, possibly because of the red hair which was a legacy from her father. She had grown to hate it herself too. Her adolescent years had been pure misery. Selfconscious and painfully thin, she had despaired of ever growing a visible bust and acquiring boy-friends like the other girls.

Naturally academic, she did extremely well at school, but her mother wouldn't let her go to university. Instead she took a course in shorthand and typing and got a job in a small manufacturing office. The woman over her was dour and in her fifties, so even at work she was repressed. She never heard any conversation about dating and boys, never learned how to apply make-up or dared buy anything but the sensible clothes her mother considered suitable.

She was seventeen when she met Trevor. She took her packed lunch into the park in summer, and after a few days of passing each other, Trevor began to smile and then to share her bench while she ate. He took her to his home to listen to records and watch the television, and she began to stay for meals.

It was all wonderful—unlike anything she had ever known, and she discovered the heady delight of feeling she was attractive to someone—of having a boy-friend at last like other girls and being kissed in the dusk on the way home. Trevor even began to hint at them getting married one day, and she was nearly delirious with joy, hardly able to believe that he could really love her.

Lauren's lips twisted, remembering. The ones who changed boy-friends every week would never have fallen for Trevor's routine. But she had.

She clenched her hands suddenly and got up to make herself a cup of coffee. Usually she tried to stop herself re-living those events seven years ago—the disillusion and the lonely terror, but sometimes memory seemed to build up until she had to give it release.

Trevor's parents had gone to visit relatives and they had been alone in the house for the first time. She hadn't been in any way nervous—it hadn't occurred to her that there was any reason to be until Trevor began to kiss her. It was different from the other occasions— there was a feverish excitement in him that frightened her, but when she protested he began to get angry and told her she couldn't really love him if she wouldn't let him do what he wanted.

She was so ignorant and naïve in those days that she only half realised what he meant at first. When he made it plain she was shocked and horrified, but mixed with the shock was the dread of losing him and everything that had suddenly given her life meaning. Sensing the weakness, Trevor played on it, blackmailing with half veiled threats, coaxing with promises that everything would be all right. Nothing would happen, he assured her, and even if it did they could get married.

Lauren wanted to believe him, but some instinct made her doubt, and when he pulled her down on to the floor her reluctant acquiescence fled. Panic-stricken, she struggled wildly, not realising in her inexperience that she had left her opposition too late. Ignoring her frenzied denial, he overpowered her, and she was forced to suffer the pain and humiliation of his clumsy, brutal haste. Luckily it was quickly over, but it left her hysterical and shamed to the core of her being.

She didn't tell anyone what had happened. It was unthinkable to even contemplate telling her own mother, and she doubted if Trevor's mother would believe her. Feeling valueless and besmirched, she hugged her secret uncleanness inside and went through each day in a vacuum.

It was nearly two months before she admitted to herself that she might be pregnant, and the time before Mandy's birth was a blur to her even now. She supposed her mind must have blanked off to save her sanity. Eventually she went to Trevor's mother. That night was the one clear thing in her memory—all of them sitting round a table and Trevor's parents saying he must marry her. Lauren agreed, unable to think of anything except that her pregnancy would soon be obvious to everyone. Her despair was complete when a few days later Trevor disappeared.

He joined the Navy, and it was only then that she fully comprehended that she had never meant a thing to him, that he had seen her blind adoration only as an opportunity to gain sexual experience. The knowledge shrivelled her inside and she discovered a depth of bitterness in herself she could never have imagined.

After Mandy was born she went back to the Munros for a while, but she was uneasy there, and as soon as she could she got a job as a mother's help. It was drudgery, but in her second job she was more fortunate. Mrs Denholm took a genuine interest in her. After a while she suggested that Lauren should have her shapeless, overlong hair styled, and showed her how to pluck her heavy, dark eyebrows down to a delicate curve.

They experimented with make-up together as well, and Lauren was startled to find what a little subtle eyeliner and shadow could do for her amber-flecked eyes. Under Mrs Denholm's guidance a real beauty emerged, fine-boned and classic. Though she was still slim she had filled out after Mandy's birth and her figure was now attractively curved. She sometimes looked in the mirror and marvelled that it could be the same girl who had been so pathetically grateful for Trevor's attention.

Ironically, it was Mrs Denholm's kindness and the miracle she had wrought which forced Lauren to leave. Nervous and hyper-sensitive with all men, Lauren detected a difference in her husband's attitude. There was nothing tangible, but she sensed that he was attracted to her and it was impossible for her to stay.

She concocted a reason for leaving, but Mrs Denholm cut her off, saying simply, 'I know.' Suddenly brisk, she got to her feet. 'I know you can't stand men at any price, and to be fair to Geoff I don't think for a single moment that he'd try anything, but it's no use closing our eyes to the fact that it's there. You're ten years younger than me and better looking. You'd be a temptation to most men.'

Helpless with embarrassment, Lauren said, 'I feel terrible. You've done so much for me—more than I could ever make you understand.'

The other woman smiled in frank self-derision. 'I enjoyed it. I lead a pretty useless life on the whole, but with you I feel I've achieved something.' Her tone becoming practical, she went on, 'What will you do now? Mandy's ready for school.'

'I'd like office work again,' Lauren admitted. 'The difficulty will be the hours.'

'Leave it with me,' Mrs Denholm told her. 'I may have the answer.'

The answer was Ann. She had worked for the Denholms when her marriage first broke up and they had kept in touch. Born in London, she was homesick and moved back, and she wanted someone to share the child care and expenses of a flat. She and Lauren liked each other on sight and Lauren immediately moved in. The bedroom they shared smelled mustily of damp and the archaic bathroom was used by all the tenants, but still it was home, and in Ann she found her first real friend of her own age.

As soon as she was settled in they both found jobs, Ann in a nearby pub and Lauren in the typing pool at Fenmore's.

She was desperately nervous before the interview. Her previous employers had known in advance that she was an unmarried mother, and Lauren wondered if she ought to tell them at Fenmore's. The mere idea made her feel sick. The searing shame she had lived through, her mother's screaming accusations, other people's embarrassment as they stumbled over whether to address her as Mrs or Miss—everything seemed to crowd in on her as she sat in the waiting room. When she was finally called in the decision was taken out of her hands. She demonstrated her shorthand and typing, gave names for references and was outside again before she could draw breath.

Though she was always haunted by the fear of discovery, the omission never caused any trouble, and no one at work suspected that she was anything but what she seemed.

Fenmore's was a new world to her. Her time in the manufacturing office was no education for it, nor could the portly Mr Phillips in any way prepare her for Warwick Sinclair. The girls in the pool were in ecstasies over him and Lauren learned all about his love affairs whether she wanted to or not. She passed him in the corridor a few times, but she never had a more personal view of him until he sent down for someone to do some typing for him. Most of it was merely copying, but one involved working out some prices, and he watched her for a while, then asked, 'Don't you need a calculator?'

Lauren shook her head. 'Not for this.'

Looking at him uncertainly, she was surprised when he smiled, the expression lighting up his rather formidable features.

'I thought they'd taken over from brains completely,' he commented. 'It seems I was wrong.'

He asked her about her shorthand and gave her several letters. She was a quick, accurate typist and he gave a small nod of approval as he signed them. She worked for him for two days until his secretary came back, quietly getting on with what she had to do and seldom speaking except in reply. She was nervous but she managed not to show it, and at the end of the second day he asked, 'What are you doing in the typing pool? You're over-qualified, surely?'

'Working,' she answered calmly. The single word on its own sounded impertinent, so she smiled. Until then she had behaved with her usual reserve, and now she caught a sudden, arrested expression as he looked at her. It was gone as quickly, and the following day she was back in the big, noisy office downstairs. By accident she discovered that Warwick had asked for her specifically, but though he sometimes spoke to her when they passed in the corridor, her brief span upstairs made no other difference.

She had almost forgotten it when he sent for her six months later. His secretary was leaving and he offered her the job. Completely taken by surprise, Lauren stammeringly refused.

His frown told her her reply was totally unexpected, and abruptly he asked, 'Why?'

There were two good reason, but Lauren couldn't tell him outright. The first was that she knew she would sometimes be required to work late, which was impossible for her, but second and more important was the common knowledge that he enjoyed more than just a working relationship with his present secretary.

Her instincts prickled a warning, and she searched for some polite excuse. Even now she sometimes had to walk away in shops or bus queues because a man, no matter how innocently, had stood too close. Her flesh crawled at the mere idea of physical contact of any kind. Beneath his formal manner and expensive three-piece suits, Warwick Sinclair was aggressively male. He was also an unashamed womaniser, and any approach he made would be far from innocent.

He was watching her steadily, and regaining her composure, she said, 'There would be times when you needed me to work late and I'm afraid I couldn't.'

'A disadvantage,' he commented. 'It's seldom more than a couple of hours. Couldn't you manage that?'

Lauren found herself considering. Ann didn't work Tuesday and Thursday evenings, but she had a boyfriend and she liked to go out. Still, if she was warned in advance and it didn't happen too often. . .

Half reluctantly she admitted the two days, and Warwick said, 'I suggest we give it a month's trial and see how it works out.'

There was nothing for Lauren to do but thank him and try to ignore the uncomfortable warning feeling which still persisted. She rose to her feet and he said, 'We'll negotiate your salary at the end of the month. You start on Monday. I'm afraid you'll only have a week with Miss Hamilton, but I realise it's not long enough and I shan't be hard on you.'

As it turned out she had not a week but a day. Reporting on Monday in her best cream shirt and brown skirt, she picked up an atmosphere immediately. Warwick and Myra Hamilton were rigidly polite with each other—too polite, and half an hour before it was time to leave, Myra, growing steadily more tight-lipped, got to her feet and marched into his office. Lauren heard the note of her voice getting higher and higher and Warwick's raised in return, then there was a loud crash and Myra came storming out, her long-lashed eyes spilling tears of rage. Snatching up her coat and bag, she disappeared through the door without a word.

Lauren sat with her downcast eyes fixed firmly on her notebook. Warwick had arrived in the doorway at the finale of the dramatic exit, but his feelings concerning it she definitely did not wish to know.

There was a long silence and he said finally, 'Miss Hamilton will not be coming back.'

Somehow Lauren muddled through the next three weeks. She was forced to ask constantly for help, but Warwick displayed a patience she later learned was not characteristic of him, and slowly she made some sort of order of what she was doing. Generally he was pleasant with her, and when he was short-tempered he was at least quite impartial and she would hear the other departments getting their share as well. On the few occasions when he had a burst of rage and his language with the offender became colourful he slammed the door between them.

At the end of the month Lauren admitted to herself that she liked working for him. The job was interesting and stimulating, and though she sometimes glanced up to find Warwick watching her, there had been no hint of the behaviour that had earned him his reputation.

Only twice during this period did he ask her to work late. The first time was a Monday, and she felt her heart sink despairingly.

'I'm sorry,' she said, not looking up, 'I can't.'

He had been in a dangerous mood all day, making her edgy, and she knew his lips would be tightening. 'Boy-friend?' he asked curtly.

Equally brief, she said, 'No.'

'If it's dressmaking or pottery you can give it a miss!'

'It's nothing like that.' In a moment he would ask what the reason was and she went on hurriedly, 'I could come in an hour earlier in the morning if it would help.'

He paused, then said, 'All right. Be ready to start at eight.'

She was there before him and ready at five to, so on that occasion she successfully got over it. The next time he was catching a late plane to Manchester and would not be in the following morning, so her offer to come in early was rejected. She began to apologise, but he cut her off and strode back to his office, slamming the door with a force that shook the walls. When she got in the next day she found pages of notes and a tape full of instructions, and wondered if she had lost her chance of the job.

At the end of the month she waited fatalistically for his decision. She knew she was satisfactory as far as her work went. The muddle at the beginning had been his own fault. Acidly, she thought he should keep his secretaries out of his bed, then he wouldn't have emotional females walking out on their jobs. She would be disappointed if he didn't keep her on. He wasn't easy to work for—he generated a tension in her, and she was continually wary, always keeping an aloof barrier between them, but she was far happier up here, doing a job that occupied her brain as well as her fingers.

It was nearly five o'clock when he sent for her and she suspected that it appealed to him to stretch her nerves. He motioned for her to sit down, then leaned back in his swivel chair and regarded her with a faint smile. 'Well, Miss Peters, your month will be up in . . .' he checked his watch, 'seven minutes' time. What is your verdict?'

'What is yours, Mr Sinclair?' she countered.

'I wonder if mine is as relevant?'

It was said musingly, but Lauren felt there was a spark of anger behind the words. 'Occasionally I wondered which of us was on probation.' Warwick paused, swinging his chair from side to side, then added deliberately, 'Have your maidenly fears been set at rest?'

Lauren flushed scarlet, unable to reply, and he waited for a moment, then went on smoothly, 'Then I presume I pass.' Picking up his pen, he tapped it on the desk while he studied her. 'Well, as to my own verdict, I think we managed very reasonably, don't you? After the rather unfortunate initial period, of course.' His dark eyes narrowed in a smile and he said softly, 'And I've no doubt you laid the blame for that squarely where it belongs.'

Her colour fluctuated again and she knew he was amused by her confusion. It seemed sometimes as though he set out to challenge her, deliberately goading to try to make her lose her cool, correct manner.

Still watching her, he lit a cigarette, then asked, 'Do you agree we should make it permanent?'

She took a deep breath. 'As long as you're quite satisfied you can manage without me working late.'

'That we shall have to cope with as it comes up. I admit I'm not keen on late-night taping sessions, but it's only happened once during the last month, so I can probably survive it.'

'In that case I should like to make it permanent,' Lauren said quietly.

'Good,' he returned. 'Now for your salary.' The sum

he proposed left her dazed and he added, 'It will be back dated to when you first came up here.'

Lauren swallowed. 'That will be very satisfactory.'

'Then I'll see you on Monday.' He checked his watch again. 'It is now exactly five o'clock.' Lauren looked at him warily, suspecting mockery, but he only said, 'Have a good weekend.'

Lauren rushed for her bus, planning what she would do with the extra money. A new television first to replace their secondhand wreck which gave out a fuzzy and unreliable image, and a new suite for the front room. Ann when she heard about it, uttered a word of caution about committing too much of her salary to rental and hire purchase, but for once Lauren was reckless and went out and arranged it all the following day.

'You don't think your boss might like a smart new dress for the office?' Ann enquired.

'I'm not there for decoration,' Lauren retorted. She had kept her clothes low key this last month—shirts that buttoned primly up to the neck and nothing that could draw attention to her figure. She might have been lulled by Warwick's manner, but she still wasn't convinced.

She wore a dress Sheila Denholm had given her on the Monday, and Warwick raised his eyebrows at her as he went through, seeming to signify approval. Lauren had a sharp return of that sensation of warning, but though he occasionally called her Lauren when they were alone, his attitude in the main was unchanged. She dreaded him asking her to work late, but it was six weeks before the need arose, and fortunately it was a Tuesday.

They worked solidly until gone seven, then Warwick stretched and said, 'That ought to do it. I shan't be in most of tomorrow, so you'll have a peaceful day to make up for it.' He lit a cigarette absently, then held the packet towards her. 'Do you smoke?'

Lauren shook her head.

'No vices at all?'

'I expect so,' she said with a faint smile. 'You tell me.'

'Being correct to a fault?' he offered.

Evenly, she asked, 'Is that a vice?' and he shrugged.

'It's debatable. Philosophers preach that the only true virtue is moderation, so in their book an excess of anything becomes a vice.'

'I wouldn't have thought so in this case,' Lauren said coolly.

She glanced up to find him watching her. He gave a slow, considering smile, then said, 'Oh, I don't know.'

There was suddenly a subtle difference in the atmosphere, and Lauren froze inside. It was only a shading in tone and expression, but Warwick had told her plainly that he was regarding her as a woman. With magnified awareness she realised they were alone in the huge building and the sky outside had darkened to nearly black. To dispel the uncomfortable sense of intimacy she briskly cleared off her desk and covered her typewriter.

Beside her, Warwick picked up his pens and slipped them into his inside pocket. Studiedly casual, he said, 'Well, I'm going to find somewhere to get a meal. Would you like to join me?'

Her heart seemed to stop, then resume with an erratic beat. This was what she had been dreading and trying by her manner to avoid. She shook her head and made her voice sound normal. 'It's very kind of you, but I'd better get home.' Crossing the room, she took her coat from the cupboard, but when she turned to leave his voice stayed her.

With an edge to his tone he said, 'Would you have worked on for another hour if I'd asked you to?'

Lauren hesitated for a moment. 'I suppose so.'

'Then have dinner with me. That needn't take more than an hour.'

She stared at him. He had pushed her into a corner and there was no way out. She felt a wave of resentment because he had forced into the open what he knew she had been at such pains to obscure. Tightly and distinctly, she said, 'I know what dining out led to with your previous secretary, Mr Sinclair. The answer is no to both!'

CHAPTER THREE

EVERYTHING changed from that moment. Lauren made few mistakes, but those she did Warwick fastened on viciously. In a good mood he was terse and unsmiling—in a bad one he blistered her.

Covering her hurt feelings, Lauren tried to ride it out, but she finally admitted to herself that the new television and the suite would have to go. She couldn't take any more of it.

She was taking her mother's engagement ring to be valued when the idea occurred to her and she tried it on. Would Warwick's pride be salvaged if he believed she was in love with someone else? Anything was worth a try.

She wore the engagement ring next day and Warwick noticed it within seconds. His voice sharp, he asked, 'When did this happen?'

'Last night,' she replied, fighting to keep a tremor from the words.

'Indeed?' He leaned back against the desk and stared down at her, his expression openly insolent. 'We're not so untouchable as we like to appear, then!'

She didn't say anything, and he waited for a moment by her desk, then slammed into his own office. For the rest of the morning he was worse than Lauren had ever known him, and at lunchtime she walked out.

Creeping in early the next morning to retrieve some things she had forgotten, she was appalled to find him already there. Her resignation in her hand, she halted, speechless, and as though nothing had happened he ordered coolly, 'Get your notebook and bring it in.'

Somehow she found herself obeying him. He dictated for two hours with only one pause while he went into her office, then said calmly, 'I shall be out for the rest of the day, so you can leave those in the folder.'

With a nod he picked up his briefcase and was gone. When Lauren went back to her office her resignation was missing from her desk and she found it torn neatly and symmetrically into four pieces in her wastepaper basket.

After that, even at his worst Warwick was just about bearable, and the only thing Lauren found hard to take was his habit of standing too close to her. He had quickly discovered that it disturbed her, but as he never attempted anything more she steeled herself to ignore it. Eventually he would either tire of it or it would cease to affect her. By now the Vivians and the Petras were on the phone daily. His spare time was obviously well filled, so she found it hard to explain why she was still so strained in his presence.

Squeals of laughter from Mandy and Sarah in the front room banished Lauren's abstraction and brought her back to the present. Sighing, she pulled the typewriter towards her. With Warwick in his current unpredictable mood, if he didn't get Monsieur Rouillière's notes in the morning, the decision on whether to go or stay might not be hers.

She typed steadily until it was time to give the girls their bath and get them to bed, then made herself a quick snack and carried on. It took longer than she had expected and, tired, she went to bed before Ann got home.

She still felt lethargic the next morning, and Warwick commented on it when he got in. Surprisingly, for once he was late. Knowing his lifestyle, it had always annoyed Lauren that he was so alert in the mornings.

Most of his girl-friends seemed to ring from their beds if it was before ten o'clock.

She managed to have the copies ready for him when he arrived, but that was the only good thing about the morning. Just after nine she'd had Petra on the phone, bright and cheerful and asking for Rick. Lauren tried to think of him as Rick and failed. It didn't fit the man she knew. With sinking heart she remembered his instructions about Petra and nerved herself to deliver the blow. Granted he had only told her to say he wasn't available, but she couldn't face the thought of doing it for the rest of the day. It was kinder to get it over with, so casually, she asked, 'Where are you at the moment?'

There was a muffled giggle. 'To tell you the truth, I haven't got up yet.'

What better place to hear it? Lauren thought, and took a deep breath. 'Petra, he *isn't* in at the moment—I haven't seen him myself yet, but . . .' Her voice trailed off. There wasn't a kind or tactful way of putting it, and she finished lamely, 'You told me yesterday you would rather know.'

There was a long silence, then Petra, oddly dignified, said, 'Yes—yes, I would. Thank you for telling me. Give him a message from me, will you?'

'Of course,' said Lauren, knowing it was probably a lie.

'Just tell him I'd have thought more of him if he'd done it himself,' Petra said simply.

'Amen to that,' Lauren said aloud, putting the phone back. She heard Warwick come in and twisted round in her chair.

He looked down at her with a frown and remarked, 'You look a wreck this morning. Are you ill?'

'Not as far as I know,' Lauren returned, smarting. 'Just a bit tired.' She paused. 'That was Miss Scott on the phone.'

'And?' he said, skimming through the mail.

'I implied that her services were no longer required,' Lauren told him bluntly.

Apparently unmoved, he said, 'Thank you,' adding, 'I hope your implication wasn't too veiled, or she might not have understood.'

'She was upset,' Lauren informed him with a surge of dislike.

He slit open the letter he was holding and commented cynically, 'She'll get over it.' Feeling her silent censure, he glanced up from what he was reading. 'Don't waste your sympathy. She's little more than a high-class prostitute.'

'That's unwarranted!' she exclaimed sharply.

He sighed. 'All right, think of some more acceptable term for a woman who hires herself out for gain. Petra makes a very good living, never fear. Her bank balance would make yours look sick.'

Only half convinced, Lauren said, 'That's not the point I was trying to make.'

She glared at him in irritation as his eyes returned to the letter and he said abstractedly, 'I know. You were concerned for her tender feelings.' He flung the letter down on her desk. 'Write and tell him to get lost. In your usual polite phraseology, of course.'

She tightened her lips and removed the letter to the other side of her typewriter. Warwick glanced down at her, taking in her expression, and said, 'I won't scandalise you with the details of our arrangement, but I can assure you that Petra knew exactly where she stood. And whatever impression she gave you, she also knew it was finished. To put it in perspective, imagine how much compunction she would have felt in dropping me if she'd found herself a Greek shipping millionaire.'

Very little, Lauren admitted, though she wouldn't say so to Warwick.

'Lauren,' he said plaintively. When she looked up, he said, 'She giggled.'

With an effort she kept herself from smiling as he went towards his office. In the doorway he turned and added softly, 'In bed.'

It wasn't really funny, she told herself determinedly as she sorted through the rest of the mail. And it didn't alter the fact that Warwick was a rat where women were concerned. Belatedly it registered that he had called her Lauren for the first time in months, and her spirits lifted. Perhaps there was a chance after all that they could get back on to their old footing.

Warwick came back and stood looking over her shoulder for a while. 'Anything urgent?'

She shook her head. 'Not desperately.'

'Have you done the copies of the notes?' Lauren silently handed them over and he put them in his briefcase. 'Right. I shan't be back until lunchtime tomorrow, so take the rest of the day off.'

Startled, she said, 'Why?'

He surveyed her critically. 'I know I have a reputation here as a slavedriving ogre. I don't need you going round with circles under your eyes to confirm it.'

'Thank you,' she snapped. 'You do wonders for my self-esteem!'

He grinned and went out, and Lauren sat for a moment looking at the things on her desk, then suddenly swept everything out of sight and put her coat on. She'd lived in London for two years and never even been round the National Gallery. The average tourist probably knew the city far better than she did.

She got the lift down and dropped in on Meg to say there would be no reply from upstairs for the rest of the day. There was a more relaxed atmosphere in the whole building when they knew Warwick was out, and Meg had a half-eaten doughnut on the table beside her and was in the mood to gossip.

'How come lover boy's given you a holiday?' she demanded. 'He's never done the same for me.'

'He thinks it's bad for his image to have me going round looking as though I'm worked to death,' said Lauren, moving the doughnut and perching on the edge of the table. 'I did some overtime last night, so perhaps a little appreciation crept in as well.'

'Myra Hamilton used to look like that after overtime,' Meg commented slyly.

'From an entirely different cause, I assure you,' Lauren told her. 'Anyway, I was doing this at home.' Meg raised her eyebrows suggestively, and she said, 'No, he wasn't with me. And even if he was, my flatmate has a five year old daughter. I imagine that would cramp even Warwick Sinclair's style.'

'Where there's a will,' Meg quoted.

Sharply, Lauren said, 'There isn't!'

'Just as well. Your fiancé wouldn't like it,' Meg observed. 'Are you bringing him to old Marshall's shindig, by the way? None of us have seen him yet.'

'I didn't know anything about it.'

'He's retiring at the end of next month,' Meg told her. 'The rattle of the collection tin should be sounding on your floor in a couple of days. They've booked a hotel for a farewell dinner and we're all invited. Though that's still on the secret list,' she added hastily.

'Your ears will grow to the size of a rabbit's,' Lauren remarked, still annoyed by her insinuation.

'Telephonists always know everything,' Meg said with a shrug. 'It's tradition.' She was disconnecting finished calls while she talked, but then there was an incoming one and Lauren prepared to slide away. Meg caught her by the door. 'You didn't say. Are you bringing your fiancé?'

'No,' said Lauren. 'He'll still be at sea.'

She escaped and stood for a moment on the pavement outside. Perhaps she should have thought a bit harder before introducing a fictitious fiancé. It had answered the purpose with Warwick, but people kept asking when she planned to get married, and she could hardly go on like this for years and years.

She began to walk, reflecting wryly on how the others would react if they learned she had only ever had one boy-friend in her life and that had been seven years ago. She couldn't recall when she last went out in the evening. Ann was loud in her condemnation of the life she led, telling her she would turn into that abomination, the possessive mother, but even Ann, knowing the full story, couldn't completely comprehend the way she felt about men.

'So he was a louse and he went off and left you,' she said once. 'I was married to a louse who went off and left me, but I've got the sense to see they're not all the same!'

Ann admitted frankly that she and Tony had married too young and Sarah had arrived too soon. They weren't ready to cope with chronic money shortage and a small baby who cried ceaselessly in a cramped flat, and one day her husband had just disappeared. Ann had been totally shattered, but she had happy times to remember as well, and the example of parents who were still deeply in love after nearly thirty years.

Perhaps that was part of the difference, Lauren pondered. Her own childhood had been the complete opposite, her mother never losing an opportunity to prove that men were base and unreliable and only interested in one thing. And in her own case that had been only too true.

Her feet had taken her mindlessly in the direction of Trafalgar Square, and she spent the morning in the

National Gallery, emerging impressed and with aching feet. She walked slowly to St James's Park and sat on the grass by the lake eating an icecream and watching the people go by. She wondered what Warwick thought she would do with the time when he gave her the day off, and thinking of him was reminded of an irritable observation Ann had once made that he seemed to creep into everything.

He did, of course, but then he was bound to. From Monday to Friday she spent nearly half her waking hours under his influence so she couldn't avoid being affected by him. His restless energy and the latent sexuality in him forced themselves on her awareness and kept her in a continual state of nervous tension.

But over the next couple of weeks, much to her surprise, he seemed to abandon his deliberate provocation. When he came in after lunch the following day he scanned her appraisingly, noting the faint colour her afternoon in the sun had given her. 'You look better anyway,' he remarked. 'What did you do with yourself?'

She laughed. 'Went round the National Gallery and lay on the grass in St James's Park.'

His eyes creased in amusement, but he only said, 'You should do it more often,' leaving her to make what she liked of the remark as he dumped a pile of work on her desk. 'Come into my office when you've surfaced from that lot!'

For the next fortnight he worked fast and solidly on the quotation for the Rouillière enquiry. Lauren went in early most mornings, but though there were few other people in the building she wasn't tense as she was if they stayed on at night, and on the whole they were getting on together remarkably smoothly. It was Lauren herself who inadvertently ruined it. Warwick was leaning on her desk going over a query with her and by accident they both moved at once and he brushed against her arm. Too late to stop her instinctive recoil, she looked up to see his dark eyes lit with anger.

'That was unintentional and you bloody well know it!' he rasped. 'What the hell's the matter with you?'

'I'm sorry,' she said helplessly. She raised her shoulders in a despairing gesture. 'It isn't only you.'

'I know. I've watched you.' He pushed himself away from the desk and stared down at her broodingly. 'It's only some men, though, isn't it, and it's got nothing to do with age either. You wince away from the kid in Accounts and the head of Sales. I've seen you do it. And me, of course, so what do we all have in common?'

She could only gaze at him and she saw his eyes narrow suddenly. 'I get it,' he said with comprehension. 'You see us as men, but the others you don't—they're just people. That's the difference, isn't it?' He gave a short, harsh laugh. 'I'm beginning to think you were designed by nature as a malicious joke!'

'A joke?' she repeated.

He flung away and paced round the office, then came back to stand in front of her. 'Well, aren't you? A beautiful, desirable woman who hates men? What else can you be except some sort of joke?'

Lauren began to cry soundlessly, the tears sliding down her neck into her collar. 'You're right,' she said at last. 'I am.'

He groaned, 'Oh, God,' and took a quick stride towards her, his hand outstretched, then stopped in frustration. 'I suppose if I laid a finger on you even now you'd run!'

'I expect so,' she agreed drearily.

Watching her, his face hardened again and he said savagely, 'Then you'd better take that ring off your finger and give it him back! The poor fool can't realise what he'll be getting!'

They were back to square one after that. Urged on by

Ann's scornful impatience, Lauren signed on at an agency to find another job, though she realised it would be hard to get the same money. She had a couple of interviews, but she was determined not to let Warwick stampede her into just any job, and she still hadn't found one when they came to the retirement dinner for Mr Marshall of Accounts.

Lauren did her best to avoid it. It was on a Friday, which was inconvenient anyway as it would mean Ann changing her night off with someone else, but in the end she felt obliged to go. She liked the elderly accountant, and it seemed everyone else in the whole firm would be there. He was a nice old man, unfailingly gentle and courteous with everyone, and she was afraid he might notice her absence.

Transport for the event proved difficult. In the end she begged a lift from Meg and her husband, and waited nervously outside for them at half past seven. Ann was reading to the two girls in their bedroom to keep them out of the way, but they were both sulking because they had wanted to see Lauren go. Mandy had been entranced and disbelieving when she saw her in the long cream dress, her bright hair waving loosely round her shoulders instead of confined in the wooden clasp.

Awed, she said, 'You look like a fairy or a princess, not like my mummy at all.'

Lauren had smiled, but truth to tell she felt unreal. The dress was another Mrs Denholm had given her, and she sent her silent thanks for her generosity as she gave herself a final check in the mirror. If she'd had to buy a dress it certainly wouldn't have been anything like the costly creation she was wearing now. It flattered her, and the knowledge that she was looking at her best gave her the confidence to face what she suspected might be an uncomfortable evening. Most of the others would be with partners, and she was nervous going on her own. But at least she didn't look as though she was alone because no one wanted her. What had Warwick called her? Beautiful and desirable. She had never thought of the irony of it until he pointed it out.

Meg and her husband were late, then they had difficulty finding the hotel, but when they eventually arrived everyone was still at the pre-dinner drinks stage. Someone thrust one into Lauren's hand—she wasn't sure what it was and she didn't particularly like it, but by holding it she avoided having anything else pressed on her. She wasn't used to drinking and she was afraid of its effect on her. Except for the bottle of sherry Ann always brought home at Christmas she hadn't tasted it since she was at the Denholms'.

Already feeling awkward because she was by herself, she tried to appear poised as she circulated among the various groups. She got several whistles of appreciation from the men in the different departments, but all the time she had the uncomfortable sensation that she was being stared at.

Casually turning to stand with her back to the wall, she fingered the zip behind her neck to make sure it was securely in place, then realised her instinct hadn't been at fault. From the other side of the room she caught Warwick's dark gaze fixed on her. Because of his height he stood out over the heads of the others, and his eyes held hers for a moment before she looked away.

Afterwards, conscious of a prickle down her spine, she refused to glance in his direction, and she was thankful when they were called into the dining room. The general talking and shuffling was interrupted by a call for silence for the Chairman to say grace, then all eyes were focussed on Warwick Sinclair, immaculate in his dark velvet jacket and white shirt. Lauren craned her neck to see who he had brought as his guest, but he had Mrs Marshall on one side and the wife of one of the other directors on the other. Probably none of his current girl-friends was suitable for this type of function, she thought acidly.

After the meal they had the presentation and the rather predictable speeches, and they moved back to the bar while the tables were being cleared and moved away for dancing.

Lauren carried her champagne through with her. Her glass had been constantly refilled during the meal so that she didn't really know how much she had drunk, but when she stood up she realised she was slightly lightheaded. It was an odd sensation she had never experienced before, not entirely unpleasant, though she felt it could easily become so if she drank any more. Reaching out occasionally to take a sip while she talked, she was surprised to find that in spite of her intentions she had managed to get more than halfway down the glass. Turning to replace it, she resolved not to have any more, then jumped to find Warwick behind her.

Her startled movement spilled the champagne over her fingers and Warwick took the glass from her. Taut and unsmiling, he held her gaze for a moment, then deliberately drained it, and leaning over until his mouth was by her ear, muttered, 'Leave it alone—you've had enough!'

Lauren flushed quickly, a mixture of annoyance and the knowledge that he was right, but he was already walking away from her. He reappeared a few moments later with a fruit juice. Putting it down by her elbow, he ordered in an undervoice, 'Stick to that for the rest of the evening, and keep out of trouble!'

If it had been anyone but Warwick she might have been grateful. Because it was him she was aware only of humiliation, and for some reason it made her defiant. Turning back to the others in the group, she realised they were looking at her curiously, and when they counted up the drinks for the next round, with a reckless glance towards Warwick, she told them she would have a vodka.

She saw his lips compress, and when they moved back into the main room for the dancing she regretted her brief challenge. She felt giddy, and one of the reps was showing an unwelcome attentiveness, trying to persuade her into another drink, then fetching it even after she had refused.

She managed to shake him off by going to the cloakroom, and returning to the ballroom, sat in a darkened corner wondering how long it would be before she could go home. Meg and her husband were entwined in each other's arms on the dance floor, obviously likely to stay to the bitter end. Lauren sat quietly, hoping the dizzy feeling would pass, and unaware of Warwick's presence until she heard his voice, muted but angry, demanding, 'What the hell are you trying to prove?'

'Why?' she asked, twisting to look up at him. 'What is it to you? Or are you afraid your dignity might suffer if your secretary appears drunk and disorderly in public?'

'As my secretary I don't care if you decide to strip and dance on the table!' he retorted, suppressed temper making his mouth grim. 'I'm not responsible for your actions! It's you I was thinking of, you stupid little fool! Are you determined to drink yourself witless?'

Her defiance draining away, she muttered defensively, 'Most of the others aren't exactly teetotal.'

Briefly she met his hard stare, then looked away quickly as he said contemptuously, 'The salesmen and the brainless little birds in the pool? On Monday they'll all be laughing and boasting about who had the biggest hangover, but you won't. I know you, and if you make a fool of yourself you'll shrivel up and die from embarrassment afterwards.' He slid a hand under her elbow, half lifting her to her feet. 'Come on out of here. I'll get you some coffee.'

This time she was grateful, and glad of the support of his arm as they threaded their way through the crowd. Near the door their progress was halted by the persistent salesman, who tried to detach her, exclaiming, 'So here you are! I've been looking everywhere for you!' but Warwick's hand tightened under her elbow. For a moment the two men faced one another, then the salesman fell back muttering under Warwick's glacial stare, and they continued to the residential lounge.

Warwick ordered her coffee black and watched while she drank it, then asked abruptly, 'Do you want to go home?'

Lauren nodded, and he said, 'I'll take you. Who had you arranged to go with?'

'Meg and her husband.' As he got to his feet she protested halfheartedly, 'You'll never find her in all that crush.'

He merely gave her an impatient glance, and when he had gone she wondered what Meg would make of the information that he was taking her home. Very few people had left so far and those only the older ones, so the telephonist would have a field day with her reputation. Lauren was vaguely surprised to find that at the moment she didn't really care. She knew that some people drank to forget their worries. Apparently it worked.

Warwick waited while she collected her coat, then steered her outside into the darkness, and strangely she had no desire to pull away from the hard grip under her arm. More important seemed her sudden thought that she was taking him away from a duty. As head of the firm he would be expected to stay longer, but when she voiced her doubts he said irritably, 'I've paid for the damned affair! They'll have to be satisfied with that!'

'That's arrogant,' she told him, still in the grip of a curious detachment. She caught her heel in a paving stone and stumbled against him, and his other hand shot out to save her.

He held her, steadying her, and on a note of anger muttered, 'Yes, you'd have to be drunk or anaesthetised, wouldn't you, before I was allowed to lay a hand on you!'

It was dark, the side street where they were standing only dimly lit, and with an exclamation he suddenly pulled her into a doorway. She went unresisting, and he hesitated, searching the pale blur of her face, then muttered, 'Oh, what the hell! What can I lose?' and kissed her.

She neither responded nor tried to escape. She was fully aware of the hard pressure of his lips, the tight hold of his arms round her back, but she was totally taken up with wonder because nothing prompted her to struggle. With an astonishment amounting to shock she realised the revulsion wasn't there.

How long the kiss lasted she had no idea. Eventually Warwick drew away and his hands slid up to hold her face, turning it towards the faint illumination of the street lamp. She heard his sharp intake of breath, then he said harshly, 'I don't know what the hell you've been playing at, but one thing is certain! You're no more engaged than I am!'

CHAPTER FOUR

SHE heard him, but she was in too much confusion to examine his words as he dragged her, almost running, to the car. Unlocking it, he thrust her ungently inside and turned to look at her for a moment before starting the engine.

'Somewhere between drunk and sober there's a point where I'll get some real answers out of you,' he told her grimly. 'And I'm going to find it!'

The car shot forward, jerking her head back against the rest. Resentful of his rough handling, she wanted to tell him she wasn't drunk. Drunken people fell over and spoke in slurred voices and were embarrassing. In her mind she said, 'The Leith police dismisseth us.' It seemed to come out quite clearly, which proved she was sober, but when she went to tell Warwick she found she had an uncontrollable desire to sleep. Her eyelids drooped and he suddenly exclaimed, 'Oh, no, you don't! You're not passing out on me now!'

He stopped the car and pulled her out. She found herself standing on a broad grass verge, and relentlessly Warwick forced her to start walking. When she whimpered that her shoes were hurting her he took them off, and the heavy dew immediately soaked through her tights and the hem of her dress. She tried to gather up the folds of the skirt in her free hand—it was so pale it would be ruined if she got it dirty.

Stumbling, she trod on something sharp and felt a ladder run up her tights. Her legs were beginning to ache from the pace Warwick set, and she pulled protestingly against his inexorable hold, saying breathlessly, 'Please, Warwick—that's enough! I'm all right now!'

He studied her face intently, then nodded, apparently satisfied, and helped her back into the car, dropping her shoes beside her. He drove silently, shooting her quick glances from time to time, and as her head cleared, Lauren remembered what he had said and began to feel uneasy. How on earth could he know she wasn't really engaged? Worse, what did he mean when he said he intended to get some answers out of her? The statement had an ominous ring, and she speculated nervously on what the questions might be.

The car slowed down and she gathered herself, shoes in hand. If she could only make her escape suddenly enough he wouldn't have time to ask her anything. Then she realised the dark scene ahead was unfamiliar and Warwick was turning off the road down a narrow ramp. She twisted towards him in quick alarm and he said, 'Before you ask, we're going up to my apartment. We're going to talk where I can see your face.'

She said sharply, 'No!' then in more conciliatory tones, 'Mr Sinclair, it's late and I want to go home. I—I don't feel very well either.'

'You wouldn't be warned,' he said unsympathetically. 'I'll take you home later, and to set your mind at rest, I have neither rape nor seduction in mind. I prefer my women willing and sober, and at the moment you don't qualify on either count.'

In rising panic, Lauren took in the eerie shadows of the underground car park. She couldn't run away from him at this time of night when she didn't even know where she was. She would have to go with him and pray that the fog would lift from her brain and she would be able to parry his questions.

Predictably, he had the penthouse apartment, with a huge window running nearly the length of the wall. For a second she saw the city spread before her, the silver gleam of the river showing between buildings, then he pressed a switch and the long curtains slid across with a faint hiss, blotting it out.

He said, 'Give me your coat,' and handing it over unwillingly, she felt more than ever trapped when he disappeared with it. In the silence she heard him filling a kettle somewhere, then he returned and said, 'Come with me and I'll show you the bathroom. Put some cold water on your face while I'm making the coffee.'

Obediently she followed him and stood for a moment looking round at the luxury. The sunken bath was the biggest she had ever seen, and comparing it with the one at home she thought with unusual bitterness that Mandy would probably grow up believing that everyone had bright green stains where the taps dripped and tatty lino to step out on to. Warwick, of course, had expensive carpet.

Guiltily she saw that her damp feet had left discolouring marks on the long, off-white pile, then she shook herself. She was here against her will, so it was his own fault. She washed her face, then stripped off her ruined tights and washed her feet awkwardly in the hand basin, intimidated by the thought of paddling round the giant bath. Underneath one heel was a place which smarted, and when she investigated she found it was slowly oozing blood. Reluctant to stain the carpet with anything so indelible, she walked back to the lounge on her toe, pausing in the doorway to enquire distantly, 'Have you got a plaster I could have?'

Warwick asked, 'What for?' and she turned and held up her foot so that he could see for himself.

He examined it swiftly. 'Sit down I'll find you one.'

Reappearing with a tin of assorted sizes and a tube of antiseptic cream, he ordered, 'Face the other way and hold it up,' and Lauren felt him balance her leg across his knee as he dealt with the small wound. His touch was completely impersonal, his fingers cool on her skin as he pressed down the plaster. He held her ankle lightly for a moment, then said, 'There you are,' and released her.

Murmuring, 'Thank you,' she sank back against the cream leather of the couch and looked up to find him watching her sardonically.

'You're improving,' he observed. 'You're comparatively sober now but you still didn't jump back. Perhaps I should keep trying.'

He poured two cups of coffee and handed one to her. It was hot and she made it last as long as possible, feeling somehow protected with the cup and saucer in her hand. The nauseating dizziness had left her, but she knew her mind wasn't functioning clearly, and Warwick's expression was implacable. She gave up the cup and saucer reluctantly when he held his hand out for them, and watched with jumping nerves as he settled himself in the opposite corner of the settee, one leg resting indolently on the other.

'Now,' he said, reaching up to undo his tie, 'let's deal first with this phoney engagement.'

Blankly, Lauren watched him slide the tie off and unfasten the top buttons of his shirt. She found herself studying the pattern of the white embroidery down the front, but roused herself to say, 'What on earth do you mean?'

'You know damned well what I mean, but I'll spell it out for you again. You are no more engaged than I am, so why the ring and the fairy tale?'

'Don't be ridiculous,' she retorted, flushing. 'What makes you say a thing like that?'

'It's simple.' He leaned forward, one arm along the back of the settee, and said, deliberately and brutally, 'Engaged couples kiss. You don't know how to.'

It was so unexpected and humiliating that her face betrayed her. Tears started in her eyes and she turned away to hide them. It was true, of course, and with his sort of experience he would be bound to know. The memory of those few kisses from Trevor was too distant, and probably he had been too inept himself to be a good tutor.

It was useless to deny it to Warwick. He had read her face. Unable to think of anything to say, she kept her eyes fixed on her folded hands, and he asked finally, 'Why did you do it? I'm presuming it was for my benefit.'

She nodded and said with difficulty, 'It was after the time you asked me to have dinner with you. Perhaps I refused rather too—strongly, but you were unbearable afterwards. I couldn't go on working for you as you were.' She twisted the ring round on her finger. 'This was my mother's engagement ring. I was going to sell it, then I decided to wear it and see what happened.' She licked her lips and swallowed, though her mouth had gone dry. 'I thought you might accept what I'd said if you thought it was because I was already—involved with someone else.'

She raised her eyes, trying to judge the effect of her words, but his face was expressionless. Without inflection, he said, 'And it kept me at bay as well, didn't it?'

He rose and went to stand in front of her. When she tried to avert her face he put his hand under her chin. 'Perhaps I'm laying myself open again, but why should you want to do that?' He paused, then said, 'You're not indifferent to me—I've always known that, even though you've kept me at a distance. So—why?'

Lauren caught her breath, her cheeks burning. No, she wasn't indifferent to him—never had been, from the first moment when she walked into his office and felt the sheer magnetic pull which was an unconscious part of him. When other heads turned to look at him, hers had turned as well. She had watched him covertly, but still as avidly as the most impressionable junior.

She felt his fingers tighten, tilting her head further back, and stared up at him defiantly. 'You've got the sort of reputation anyone with any sense steers clear of. I knew what you expected from the women you took out.'

'Some of them,' he agreed. 'I don't pretend that with Petra it was ever a meeting of minds, but she's well travelled and she knew the score.' He smiled slightly. 'But I don't always choose my companions solely on their availability.'

'Don't you?' she challenged. 'The end result seems to be the same, in spite of that.'

He hesitated, shrugging. 'But you only had to say no. I may use persuasion, but I don't force myself on any woman.'

He wouldn't need to, Lauren thought bitterly. She had seen his charm in action often enough when he wanted something. He was undeniably handsome and he knew the power of his own sexual attraction. It was a combination powerful enough to overcome most women's defences.

His hand dropped away from her chin and he leaned forward and pulled her to her feet, still holding her with that curiously intent gaze. 'You knew I was attracted to you all along, but what's wrong with that?'

She wanted to tell him, but mesmerised, she couldn't find the words. Slowly, carefully, Warwick drew her closer, and with deliberate gentleness said, 'You only have to say no at any point.'

He bent his head and she saw his mouth coming nearer and closed her eyes. She wanted him to kiss her. With other men the revulsion had been genuine and instinctive—she shrank from them mindlessly, but with Warwick it had been another kind of fear. Something had warned her that with him it might be different, and she must never risk him getting close enough for her to find out. He was dangerous. God, she had Mandy at home to prove what could happen if she let a situation get out of her control!

But the gentle, sensual pressure of Warwick's lips as they moved on hers was so very different from Trevor's callow assault. Then she had been in love with the idea of love, not even admitting to herself that she was unmoved by what he seemed to find so exciting.

There was no comparison between her memories and what she experienced now. This she wanted. When at last Warwick lifted his head she sighed with loss. Eyes still closed, she felt a faint tremor in his fingers as they caressed round her ears, and, his voice low, he said, 'Kiss me properly, Lauren. Open your lips to me.'

His mouth returned to hers and she learned for the first time what kissing could do—that it was more heady than all the champagne she had drunk that evening, and it caused a strange movement deep within her that spread to her thighs, making her tremble. Warwick's arms tightened, pulling her against him, and momentarily she had a return of the old panic as the hard outlines of his body were impressed on her. She tensed in rejection, and his hold slackened until she gradually relaxed and the spasm of fear was replaced by a rising warmth.

Suddenly she needed to be closer still, and as he sensed it his exploration of her mouth became more urgent and one hand slid up to find her breast. She felt the heat of his fingers and the flaring response of her body where they touched. The unreasoning part of her wanted him to go on, but when he reached round to undo her zip she stiffened and jerked away.

Shaking her head, her voice strangled, she whispered, 'No, Warwick.'

It was more a plea than a demand, but he checked, then gathered her head against him. 'Let me, Lauren,' he breathed against her hair. 'Don't stop me now. You're beginning to come alive for me—I can feel it.'

She still shook her head, and he took hold of her shoulders and moved her away until he could look down at her. Searching her face, innocent of make-up and vulnerable, he swore under his breath, then with sudden decision, picked her up and carried her into the bedroom. Setting her on her feet, he retained his hold on her, shaking her slightly when she struggled. 'Don't—it's all right! I want you, God knows, but there's nothing new in that and I'm used to it.'

His eyes held hers, gazing into their frightened, golden-brown depths, and the harshness faded from his voice as he repeated, 'It's all right.' His hands moved on her shoulders, stroking the skin over the delicate bones. 'I'm only going to hold you and touch you—teach you to feel the pleasure I can give you. I won't take it all the way, I swear, even if you want me to. Trust me.'

Lauren closed her eyes, swaying. Warwick was the last man in the world she should trust, but something was happening to her—she was in emotional and physical turmoil and she could no longer reason. The flood of sensation washing through her was too intense for rational thought. She felt him undo her dress and slide it down over her shoulders until it fell about her feet, then the long waist slip followed. Holding her wrist with one hand, he threw back the quilt and lowered her to the bed.

Her pulse loud in her ears, she watched him shrug impatiently out of his shirt, watched his long fingers undo the small clasp on the front of her bra, then she closed her eyes again as he pressed himself down on her. For a while he was motionless, as though just this contact between them was sufficient. Engulfed by his weight and the leashed power of his muscled body, Lauren lay with all her senses clamouring. Warwick's warmth and the feel of the harsh hair on his chest seemed magnified on her sensitised skin, and when at last he moved and turned to seek her mouth, she slid her arms round him, locking them behind his back as though by holding him she could make time stand still and be captured in this moment for ever.

His mouth still claiming hers, he made an exultant sound in his throat, then lifted his head and trailed his lips down her neck, lingering to probe the hollow at the base with his tongue before moving down to fasten on her breast. She jerked and gasped shudderingly. Reaching out blindly, she seized his head, her fingers clutching urgently in his hair until the wave of sensation became too acute, almost pain, and she moaned and pushed him away.

He drew back and she opened dazed eyes to meet his dark, questioning gaze. His fingers kneaded her soft flesh gently, and there was a faint unsteadiness in his voice as he said, 'Have you been touched like this before, Lauren?'

Speechless from the tide of feeling he induced, she shook her head, and he ordered roughly, 'Say it.'

A catch in her voice, she whispered, 'No, never.'

Something glittered in his eyes, then his hand moved down sweepingly over her body and his mouth descended on hers again. Desire burned in her, dangerous, because it was too newly awakened to be recognised, and under the combined kindling of his lips and touch, an unbearable force built up within her. She forgot that she had ever been afraid of him, and the welling emotion in her could question nothing he did. He had shed the rest of his clothes, but it never ever occurred to her to wonder if his own control was now any greater than her own.

Lost, dissolving in a dizzy spiral of yearning, she turned and arched herself against him in mute appeal. Under her hands she felt the muscles in his back contract in instinctive response. He started to move over her, then froze, and swearing quietly and vehemently, let himself down heavily beside her.

Tremors shook her, catching in her breath, and he reached out and pulled her head down on his chest to stroke her hair, soothing her like a child until her wild pulse steadied. The first sharpness of unsatisfied desire began to fade, and he said quietly, 'I'm sorry— I took it too far. It wasn't meant to turn into a torment.'

He ducked his head to look at her, lips twisting, and moved her head until it rested over the erratic thud of his heart. 'For both of us, if that's any comfort to you.' He gave a short laugh, then his hand resumed its slow stroking. 'Even though you've been tormenting me for the last twelve months!'

Lauren stirred and raised her head. 'Not intentionally, Warwick.'

'Rick,' he corrected with a faint smile. The smile faded and his fingers tightened in her hair. 'It might not have been intentional, but you knew.' He tugged her hair again, more gently this time. 'Didn't you?'

'Perhaps, but not consciously.' She sighed. 'I only knew I should get away, but when I tried you wouldn't let me.'

'No.' There was self-derision in his voice as he said, 'When it came to the point I couldn't stand the thought of someone else sitting in your chair.' He took her face between his palms, rocking it gently. 'When I walked through your office and saw that cool little smile you gave me, I used to imagine getting you into bed with me.' He began to laugh. 'And what happens when I finally achieve it? God, how did I ever get myself into this position? I must have a latent streak of masochism! I warn you, I'm not binding myself with promises a second time!' He turned on to his side, taking her with him. 'What is it about you, Lauren Peters?'

She met the gleam of humour in his eyes uncertainly. 'I don't know what you mean.'

'No, you don't, do you?' His expression became enigmatic. 'And I don't think I'm going to tell you.' Easing himself further down the bed, he pulled the quilt up round them both. 'So put your arms round me and let's try to get some sleep. I'll get you home before it's light.'

Sleep seemed impossible to Lauren, but it came quickly. She stirred into wakefulness once and realised she had turned over and Warwick was curved round her against her back, one arm holding her slackly. A suffocating rush of pure happiness surged through her. Careful not to wake him, she moved until her entire length was touching him, deliberately fighting off drowsiness so that she could savour the closeness.

She woke next time to his hand on her shoulder. A faint grey line showed under the curtains, and he said, 'Close your eyes for a moment. I'm going to put the light on.'

She sat up and covered her eyes against the sudden brightness, her long red hair spreading round her. Warwick touched his lips to her back, then picked up one of the heavy locks and said reflectively, 'I always used to wonder if it was really this colour. Your eyebrows and lashes are dark.'

She flushed with a deep, mortified embarrassment, made worse because he was fully dressed, and hiding his amusement, he handed her a cup of coffee and two tablets.

'I imagine you're paying the penalty for the champagne, so take these. How's your head?'

It wasn't good, but the dull throb was nothing compared with the rest of her distress. The alcohol-induced euphoria was gone as though it had never been, and she tried to push back the memories that flooded into her mind, flaying her.

Trying to cover herself with the quilt, she took the coffee and tablets, but as soon as she had swallowed them, Warwick took the cup away from her.

'Stop it,' he ordered curtly.

She pressed her knuckle to her mouth in sharp hurt at his tone, and he watched her for a moment, then sat down beside her and pulled her hand away. 'Stop it,' he repeated more gently. 'All you've done is get over your hang-up and find you've got the same feelings as the rest of us. Last night was neither a sin nor a crime.'

He set the cup down on the bedside table and turned back to her, his narrowed eyes assessing. 'Look at me.'

Lauren turned her head further away and he reached out and forced it back. 'Blame me if it makes you feel any better. I started it, and I do have rather more experience than you.'

She was incapable of any reply, and he waited, still watching her, then said abruptly, 'But last night wasn't only the champagne singing in your blood, was it? There's been something between us for a long time now or it wouldn't have happened, no matter how much you'd drunk.' He took hold of her shoulders in a hard grip. 'Would it, Lauren?'

She dropped her head and twisted away again, and he said impatiently, 'Lauren! Or can't you face me because you let me see that you wanted me?'

Vividly there came the memory of the way she had implored him by her actions to take his lovemaking to its conclusion, and a dark flush stained up to her temples. No, she couldn't face him. Not now, or even worse, across the office on Monday. Curling, shrivelling inside, she heard him say tautly, 'So it is that. Then does it help you to know this?' Dragging her with him, he stood up and held her forcibly along the length of his body. 'What do you think it was like for me, holding you in my arms in that bed when I'd sworn to you that I wouldn't take you? I wanted you then and I still want you now!' With his arms locked behind her he moved deliberately against her. 'Do you need any more convincing? Does knowing what you do to me make us quits?'

Abruptly releasing her, he turned away. 'Now for God's sake get your clothes on!'

He went out, and shaken, her heart pounding, Lauren sank back on to the bed. Stone cold sober now, she should have been shocked, but instead an involuntary response had flared in her. Swallowing, she sat for a moment, then began to dress with frantic haste. In the bathroom she washed and rinsed her mouth with an antiseptic wash she found on the shelf. Her ruined tights still lay in a corner and she took them back to the bedroom, wondering rather helplessly what to do with them. Warwick came in, and without a word took them from her and tossed them into the wastepaper basket.

'What's your cleaner going to think?' she asked hesitantly.

His eyes narrowed in cynical amusement. 'That's another difference between us. I don't care.'

He held her coat for her and she slipped it on. 'Are you ready?'

She looked round nervously for anything she might have left, then nodded and followed him out to the lift. Inside, he pulled her roughly against him and kissed her. 'Stop looking like that!' As she tried to pull away his hands tightened, holding her effortlessly. 'Come out with me tonight. We'll have a meal somewhere.'

'I . . . I can't,' she stammered.

'Because it isn't Tuesday or Thursday? We never did talk, did we?'

The lift doors opened, saving Lauren from a reply, and the echoing concrete in the garage inhibited further speech. They were still silent as they emerged into the empty streets. Warwick drove slowly, keeping down the note of the Porsche's exhaust, and as they neared her flat he cut the engine and let the car coast quietly in to the kerb. Lauren had her key ready when it stopped, but he leaned over and held the door closed when she turned to get out.

Softly, he said, 'If you have any ideas about not turning up on Monday, forget them!' Observing her quick guilt, he nodded. 'Yes, I guessed you might have that in mind, but if you don't appear I'll come and fetch you!'

He meant it, and Lauren knew it was useless to argue with him. With a small shrug she got out and watched him drive away, then let herself in. To her relief Ann was asleep and she undressed hurriedly, draping her dress over a chair but letting her other things stay where they fell. She hardly seemed to have closed her eyes when the alarm went off, and resentfully she pulled the sheet over her aching head.

Ann drew it back to peer at her and returned a few minutes later with a cup of tea and the bottle of paracetamol. 'Take four-hourly for hangovers,' she said with mild sympathy. 'I take it that's what ails you?'

'Yes,' Lauren admitted.

'And presumably lack of sleep as well. I woke up at three o'clock and you weren't back then.' She waited to see if Lauren would offer any comment, then said, 'I'll keep the kids out of your hair until it's time for me to go. In return for some information.'

'What about?' Lauren enquired tiredly.

Ann looked significantly at the clothes on the floor. 'On how you go out in the evening in a pair of tights and come home without them the next morning.'

As an exit line it wasn't reassuring. Lauren still hadn't decided how much to tell her when she went into the kitchen later. Ann was swiftly and competently ironing a pile of small dresses, and she glanced up and viewed Lauren consideringly. 'On a scale of nought to ten, what was the degree of inebriation?'

'Oh, about five or six, I suppose.'

'Halfway between sober and unconscious—the dangerous stage. Who brought you home?'

'Warwick,' Lauren said unwillingly.

Ann paused, her brows lifting, then set the iron on its heel. 'From what you've told me about him, wasn't that a trifle rash on your part? And what happened to the tights, or isn't it for publication?'

'They were wrecked,' said Lauren. She sank down on a chair by the table and rested her chin on her hands. 'He marched me barefoot up and down a grass verge somewhere to sober me up.'

'Oh,' said Ann, nonplussed for a moment. Caustically, she added, 'I wouldn't have expected him to be guilty of such chivalry. Mind you, you still took a risk. You were more likely to have ended up in his bed.' She saw the colour flare swiftly in Lauren's face and drew a sudden, hissing breath. 'Oh, God, Lauren, you didn't . . .?'

Lauren shook her head quickly at her aghast expression. 'No, it's all right.' With difficulty she went on, 'It didn't go—all the way.'

Her face still blank with shock, Ann filled the kettle and switched it on, then went back to the table and sat down. 'Let's start again, and make sure I'm grasping it properly. You were in bed with Warwick Sinclair, you've admitted not entirely sober, and he didn't take advantage of the fact?'

'No.'

'You're quite sure you weren't too far gone to remember?'

Lauren shook her head. 'I wasn't that bad.'

In thoughtful silence Ann took out a cigarette. Slowly, she said, 'Well, in any man that would be unusual to say the very least. In his case I should think it must be unique.' She got up as the kettle began to boil and made the coffee. Still pensive, she carried the mugs back to the table, and said at last, 'Frankly, there's only one explanation I can think of.' She met Lauren's glance of enquiry, and said bluntly, 'He must have presumed he'd got a virgin on his hands, in which case it's faintly feasible he may have had scruples about seducing you because of the state you were in.'

Startled, Lauren looked up, her eyes widening, and the other girl said, 'It's not so surprising really. You have a virginal air. I've never come across a more unlikely unmarried mother in my life.'

Staring down into her mug, Lauren went over the previous evening. It had all started when Warwick kissed her and discovered her astonishing ignorance. And she had more or less told him she had never been made love to before. She had answered his question truthfully, but the truth had conveyed a lie. Haltingly, she said at last, 'I think you must be right.'

Ann glanced out of the window to where Mandy and Sarah were playing on the patch of grass. 'Your daughter is likely to come as a double shock,' she observed drily. She saw Lauren wince, and asked, 'Was last night just a piece of opportunism on your boss's part, or is he interested?'

'Oh, he's interested—I think I've always known that, but with Warwick Sinclair, interest only takes the one form. If he'd thought I was responsible for my own actions I'd probably be launching myself off the Embankment by now.'

Ann balanced her mug between her two hands and regarded Lauren speculatively. 'Do I presume that you were willing?'

Briefly, Lauren said, 'Yes.'

There was a short silence, then Ann said, 'Tell me to mind my own business if you like, since it's rather a personal subject, but yesterday you still jumped a mile if any man so much as sat by you.' She traced her finger along a meandering pattern on the table top. 'What I'm getting at is how come this very startling transformation from frightened rabbit to bedmate in a single hop?'

'I love him,' Lauren said flatly. 'I think I always have.'

She heard her own words without surprise, though until she spoke them aloud she had never even admitted to herself what she felt for Warwick. She met Ann's despairing regard with a small, resigned smile. 'Stupid, isn't it?'

Ann covered her face with her hands for a long moment, then sighed. 'Oh God, I've wanted you to fall in love—prayed for it, but I'm terribly afraid you've picked the wrong man.'

'I know,' Lauren said listlessly. She got up and went over to the ironing board, taking up where Ann had left off on the green cotton dress. 'You'd better get ready for work or you'll be late.'

'To hell with work!' Ann said explosively. 'Lauren, what are you going to do?'

'I don't know. I haven't thought about it yet.'

'Leave Fenmore's,' urged Ann. 'Get right away from him.'

Lauren stared without seeing at the garment under her hands. It was the commonsense thing to do, but a world without Warwick would be bleak.

'Lauren!' Ann said insistently.

'I don't know whether I've got the will power to do it.'

'But you're no match for a man like him! It's an unequal contest from the start!'

Lauren met her concerned eyes and gave a faint shrug. 'I know.'

She wanted to think, but the rest of the day was a rush and until she had put the children to bed there was no time. She lay on her own bed then and stared up at the ceiling, her stomach lurching every time she thought of going in to work on Monday. She dreaded facing Warwick, yet she still couldn't take Ann's advice.

She loved him. Looking back, she marvelled at her own blindness, at how she had accepted the excuses she made to herself for not leaving when she could have done. And what was she going to do now? Their relationship could never return to what it had been. Warwick wouldn't let it.

The thought of being added to his list of mistresses, of finding herself the subject of the lunchtime conversations at Fenmore's, made her squirm. And it had so nearly happened. If Warwick had known about Mandy it would have been a very different story, and she suspected that if he had once made love to her she would have felt there was little point in denying him afterwards.

She had escaped by a hairsbreadth, and it was up to her now to pretend that the love and need he had aroused did not exist. At least it was made easier in the one way, because she couldn't fool herself that there could ever be a happy ending. The chairman of Fenmore's would never take on anyone with such obvious proof of a past indiscretion. An apparent indiscretion anyway, because to reveal the truth would mean Mandy learning that she had been conceived in an act of violence.

She went to sleep clinging to the thought of Mandy. She would have enough to cope with when she got older—she could not, *must* not do anything which might add to the difficulties her daughter would have to overcome.

CHAPTER FIVE

On Monday Lauren was barely settled at her desk before the phone went, and she heard Meg's voice, sharp with curiosity, on the other end. Without preamble, she demanded, 'And is he as good as he's supposed to be?'

'I wouldn't know,' Lauren returned shortly.

'Oh, come on,' Meg wheedled. 'Just a hint if you're shy.'

'I can't give you even that. I've no experience either of his proficiency or lack of it.'

'Come off it,' sighed Meg in patent disbelief. 'You were floating on champagne the last time I saw you, and Warwick's not the man to pass up an opportunity like that!' She paused, then said, 'Myra Hamilton said he had one or two tricks that nearly blew her mind.'

'How gratifying for her,' said Lauren, letting her distaste show in her tone. 'But the fact remains that I reached home entirely unscathed. Perhaps I'm just not his type.' She heard footsteps coming in from the corridor and knew before his hands rested on her shoulders that it was Warwick. 'Was there anything else? I've got work to do.'

Disgruntled, Meg rang off, and Warwick lifted her hair away from her neck and lightly kissed the exposed nape. Lauren held herself still, using all her will power to prevent herself from turning to him. Lying close to him with his arms clasped round her in sleep had been the greatest happiness she had known in her life, but Meg's words had reduced it to a sordid interlude.

Warwick was still holding her hair and she leaned

forward until it was freed from his grasp. Looking down at her closed expression, he lifted his brows. 'Was Meg getting her poisonous tongue to work?'

'Yes—though she couldn't tell me anything I didn't already know.'

'Which is?'

'That a good many women, at least one of them from here, have shared your bed.' Her eyes blurred with tears and she rapidly blinked them away, suddenly overcome with revulsion at the thought that Myra and all the others might have lain where she had with Warwick.

Avoiding his eyes, she leaned forward and began to take the things out of her drawer, but he checked her, saying abruptly, 'Leave those and come into my office. Anyone can walk in on us here, but my door they'll knock.'

With a rush of unreasoning panic she exclaimed, 'No——' but he overrode her.

'Lauren, we're going to talk whether you like it or not, and it might as well be here.'

'No!' she repeated distractedly. 'I don't want to talk! I—I've got nothing to say.' She forced herself to look up and meet his gaze. 'Mr Sinclair, I——'.

He laughed, without humour, before she could get any further. Shaking his head in disbelief, he swung her chair round towards him, holding the armrests so that she was trapped, his face barely a foot away from hers. 'Lauren, you're incredible!' She stiffened and tried to back away, and deliberately and with emphasis, he went on, 'Last Friday you let me undress you. I held you, I kissed you, I touched every part of you and you went to sleep with my arms round you. Doesn't that put us on first-name terms?'

Her face burned and he demanded, 'What's the matter? Am I too direct for you? Or are you trying to pretend it never happened?'

'Yes!' she burst out. 'I *would* be incredible if I really believed it hadn't changed things, but what I was saying—what I was trying to tell you, is that I want to forget it—I want both of us to forget it! There's no other way I can go on working for you!'

She tried to push his hands away, but he only tightened them, and demanded, 'Why?'

Stonily, she said, 'For reasons which are my own and which I don't have to give you.'

'And if I tell you that I can't forget it, nor do I want to?'

Neither could she, Lauren thought despairingly. As much as she wished the memories could be wiped away, part of her insisted on recalling them, reviving the primitive feelings which had coursed through her.

Aloud, she said in a stiffly controlled voice, 'Whatever the other night may have led you to expect, I'm not going to have an affair with you.'

'I haven't asked you to. I've told you before, you only have to say no. Don't condemn me without trial. Give it a chance and form your own judgement.'

Her voice toneless, she said, 'What makes you think I might want to give it a chance?' and Warwick laughed and slid his hand down her cheek.

'I'd only embarrass you again if I answered that!'

Lauren knew what he meant and it was embarrassment enough. She was relieved when the phone rang in his office and he left her to take it. Afterwards it went endlessly, and towards break time she heard him say in exasperation, 'Meg, no more calls for the next half hour!'

He tossed the receiver back on to the rest, and Lauren winced as she always did. One day he would break it, and wanton damage offended her. Through the half open door, he called, 'Lauren, make some coffee and bring it in here!'

'Please,' she muttered under her breath, glad all the same that he seemed to be back in a working mood. When she carried the tray in he was on the intercom, a heavy frown on his face. He spoke shortly, his deep tones clipped, and when it was concluded looked up at her, still frowning. 'It's nothing but interruptions here. Have lunch with me.'

'No,' she returned, tensing again.

'Dinner, then.'

'No.'

His mouth thinned as it always did when his patience was stretched, and near desperation, she said, 'I'm just not getting through to you, am I?'

'Or I'm not.' He reached for a cigarette and lit it with a jerky, irritable movement. 'I'm only asking you to have dinner with me. It's perfectly harmless, and even the most respectable people do it all the time. All right, it's Monday, which for some reason is one of your banned days, but tomorrow I'm going to come round and park outside your damned front door and I'll sound my horn at five minute intervals until you *do* agree to come out with me!'

Lauren stared at him, helplessness and anger mixed. 'That's blackmail!'

'You're so right,' he conceded. 'Well?'

She felt a rare surge of fury at the alternatives he left her. Granted, she could walk out of here now. She could even ring the police and say he was annoying her, but going out to dinner with him was such a minor thing by comparison that she could only capitulate.

Ann was waiting for her when she got home, and Lauren was barely through the door before she said expectantly, 'Well? How did it go?'

Lauren grimaced. 'Not as planned. The reverse, in fact.' She saw Ann regarding her with frustration and gave a wry, half smile. I'm having dinner with him tomorrow.'

A quivering excitement swept through her as she spoke, bringing a faint colour to her face. Noting it, Ann said abruptly, 'You're going to get hurt.'

'Perhaps. I said I was a fool.' Lauren wiped some rain spots from her shoulder bag and dropped it back on to the table. '*Is* this being in love? I know perfectly well I should keep away from him, but I get moments when I suddenly don't care what I might be letting myself in for.'

'It's hardly likely to be a blinding attack of infatuation when you've been working for him for twelve months,' Ann pointed out with dry accuracy.

'No,' Lauren allowed, sighing. 'But I'm not sure what love feels like either. I know what I feel for Mandy, but this is different.' She paused, the need to talk warring with the long habit of guarding her thoughts. 'Perhaps I should just let it run its course. When he finishes it I shall have to accept that it was all futile anyway. If I go on keeping him at a distance I shall go on dreaming and kidding myself.'

On a sudden note of bitterness, Ann said, 'You're kidding yourself now. That doesn't work either.' She got up with a jerky movement and went to stand by the window. Startled, Lauren followed her with her eyes, and Ann gripped the sink for a moment, then turned back to face her. 'If it's love, real love, not just infatuation or a physical obsession, the only complete cure is death.' She gave a twisted smile. 'His or yours— it doesn't matter which.'

Shocked into silence, Lauren said at last, 'So it's still Tony. I didn't realise. You've never said anything before, and it doesn't show.'

Ann raised her shoulders in a disclaiming gesture. 'I thought I'd come to terms with it after five years ...'

She shrugged again and went over to the mirror, carefully blotting the tears from her eyes before they could spill over and smudge her mascara. 'Listen to the voice of experience and back off before you get in too deep.' She pulled a wry face at her reflection. 'Unless . . .'

'Unless what?'

'Well, he's known you the same length of time. I suppose it's possible . . .'

Her voice trailed off and Lauren said flatly, 'I'm too old to believe in fairy tales, and there's the small matter of Mandy.'

'Yes,' said Ann. 'And I'm not going to start up the argument again—we've been all through it often enough, but in this particular instance I have a very strong feeling that it would be better if you told him now.'

'No,' Lauren said with finality.

'He's not in any position to throw stones,' Ann pointed out.

'I know that.' Lauren hesitated. 'But for one thing, widows, divorcees and unmarried mothers are all bracketed together in men's minds. We've got nothing to lose and we're automatically presumed to be suffering from frustration.'

'And the other thing?' Ann prompted.

'He would be bound to think . . .' Lauren broke off, finding it difficult to put into words even to Ann. 'Well, he would be bound to think that the other night I was leading him on—deliberately making a fool of him, and I imagine it would be the one thing most men would never forgive.'

Ann considered, and finally agreed, 'Difficult. You're on to a loser all ways, whatever you do.'

It was a conclusion Lauren had reached herself. If Warwick kept up his present tactics she couldn't hope to hide Mandy's existence from him for long, but cowardice prompted her to delay the discovery for as long as possible.

She was aided in her decision by the fact that it was a hectically busy day at work and there was no time for a session of soul-baring. Warwick had originally said he would pick her up at eight, but he was still at his desk when she left, and with a grimace at his watch he said, 'Better make that half past.'

Lauren agreed, masking her relief. The later time cut the risk of accidental confrontation. By eight-thirty Mandy should be safely asleep. When she got home she snatched a quick bath, then washed her hair in the kitchen sink as they always did. She was blow-drying it in front of the mirror when Ann came in, her expression betraying that she couldn't make up her mind whether to be concerned or encouraging.

Finally, Lauren told her, 'Go on, say it. I'm going out with a man at last, and if it was anyone but Warwick you'd be delighted.'

Ann gave a faint, rueful smile. 'True,' she admitted. 'Though since you *are* going, I feel you should keep your end up. What are you wearing? It's safe to assume you'll be going somewhere expensive.'

'I don't know,' said Lauren, feeling a clutch of fright. The Denholms had taken her out for a meal a few times and she'd stayed at hotels with them when they went on holiday, but that was her total experience of eating out. And though they were well off they didn't come anywhere near Warwick's income bracket, so even those few occasions couldn't give her much guide as to what to expect.

'Come on,' said Ann, observing her nervousness. 'If you leave it till the last moment you'll find your shoes don't match.'

Lauren's choice was limited to the dresses Sheila

Denholm had given her, and she only had her cream or black sandals which were really suitable for evening wear. They examined the contents of the wardrobe in silence, and Ann finally drew out a black dress. 'It has to be this one, and it's got a jacket, so you've solved the problem of a coat.'

Lauren viewed it doubtfully. It must have cost a fortune, like all Sheila Denholm's clothes. Sleeveless, it was embroidered with a metallic black thread, but the crossover bodice was cut very much lower than anything she had ever worn before.

'You're not dressing for the office now, dear,' Ann said with affectionate derision. 'Try it on, and make sure it doesn't smell of damp. I wore a shirt the other night that must have been against the wall in my wardrobe and I realised when I got out that I was enveloped in a delicate aura of mildew. Fortunately Mac has practically no sense of smell.' She looked up at the telltale mottling on the wallpaper near the ceiling. 'We're going to have to do something about this bedroom one day.' Turning back to Lauren, she picked up the dress. 'Stand still and I'll put it over your head for you. You hair's still wet.'

Obediently Lauren held up her arms while Ann eased it on and zipped up the back, then slipped on her sandals and revolved slowly, watching the soft swing of the full skirt. Strangely, black was a colour she never wore, but she admitted that it did something for her. Her pale skin seemed almost translucently clear by contrast. She hoped she would get used to the fact that there was a lot more of it showing than usual.

She grew more and more nervous as half past eight approached, and, unused to her going out, Mandy played up, trying to claim her attention by alternately sobbing and sulking. It made her late, and finally Ann exclaimed in exasperation, 'For goodness' sake, leave her to me and get yourself ready! Let her cry! You must be the only mother in the land who never went out and left her child until she was six!'

It was probably true, but some of Mandy's upset communicated itself, and Lauren found her hands were shaking as she watched by the window for the Porsche. She knew Mandy was still awake and as soon as it appeared she called goodbye to Ann and let herself swiftly out before Warwick could ring the bell.

As he got back into the car after helping her in, he slid a sideways glance at her, noting her shuttered expression, and said, 'I thought I might have to come and fetch you out.' When she made no comment, he eased the car away from the kerb and added, 'I would have done.'

'Yes,' said Lauren, her tone carefully neutral. 'I guessed you would.'

'And that's the only reason you came?'

His voice had sharpened and she felt a tiny spurt of satisfaction as she said, 'Yes.' This was too easy for Warwick. He was merely taking out a woman he found attractive—something he must have done hundreds of times in his adult life. He didn't have to cope with apprehension and confused feelings and a child's tantrums. It was all very different for him.

'Your enthusiasm is flattering,' he observed ironically.

'Don't complain if coercion doesn't produce all the desired results.' She gave him a cool look. 'You knew I wasn't coming willingly, so why pretend?'

With a swift glance in the rear mirror he pulled abruptly into the side of the road, the rasp of the handbrake harsh as he applied it viciously.

'Tell me something if you're so set on being frank,' he said savagely. 'What's wrong with me? I haven't got a police record, I don't smell, my nephews and nieces don't find me repulsive and my parents' dogs are always delighted to see me!' He turned a hard stare on her and added with acid emphasis, 'And you have personal experience of the fact that I don't go in for rape!'

Lauren retreated nervously from the expression in his eyes, and finally muttered defiantly, 'Why won't you believe that I just don't want to get involved with you?'

'For God's sake!' His exclamation was explosive. 'You've got one thing in common with my niece anyway. She's five, and if she finds anything different on her plate she refuses it automatically on the grounds that she knows she's not going to like it because she's never had it before!'

'So I'm childish,' Lauren said distantly.

He took a deep breath. 'There's a certain similarity in attitude.' He shifted in his seat and half turned towards her, his arm across the steering wheel, fingers splayed out on the rim. 'And you don't know what you're talking about when you say so glibly that you don't want to get involved.'

'I can hazard a guess,' she retorted.

For an instant his lips tightened. 'We've been into this before. I haven't concealed the fact that I've wanted you for a long time now. Yes, I'd make love to you if you were willing.'

'Willing and sober,' she said pointedly.

His dark eyes narrowed dangerously. 'I was a bloody fool that night. I could have stopped all this argument, and a couple more drinks and you'd got it coming to you anyway.'

She looked across at him in quick puzzlement. 'What do you mean?'

'I thought so,' he said with derision. 'You don't even know what I snatched you out of, do you? My dear innocent, why do you think Richardson, the Lothario of Sales, was plying you with vodka? He was hanging round you like a dog guarding a particularly succulent bone! God, he was nearly ready to take *me* on for you! He was only waiting for you to get to the stage where you didn't know which way you were pointing and he'd have gallantly offered to run you home. It shouldn't take too much imagination to guess where you'd have ended up.'

'I know where I did!' she flashed.

For a brief moment his anger surfaced. Bitingly, he said, 'Be grateful I don't operate the same principles!'

'I'm sorry,' she muttered. 'You're right—I hadn't realised, so I didn't know you were being quixotic. Though . . .' She checked, feeling his eyes on her. She had been about to say she would need to be unconscious before she allowed Carl Richardson anywhere near her, but she suddenly realised the admission she would be making. Still, she was uncomfortably certain that Warwick had picked up her thoughts. The grimness faded from his mouth and his expression was almost goodhumoured as he started up the engine again.

When they arrived at the restaurant, Lauren was relieved to discover it was a small one. The entrance was up a steep flight of narrow stairs and faintly shabby, but inside it was richly carpeted, the plain apricot linen on the walls adorned with prints of old cartoons. Clearly they intended to limit their clientele to the discriminating.

Warwick was obviously well known, and a discreet waiter slipped Lauren's jacket from her shoulders while he was ordering drinks. She went ahead of him and sat where he indicated in a small alcove off the bar. He slid in beside her on the velvet-covered seat and the waiter straightened up the long table in front of them so that they seemed enclosed in their own small world, cut off from the rest of the room.

Lauren was immediately uncomfortable. It felt strange and wrong for Warwick to be sitting beside her in these circumstances. The transition from their relationship of a few days ago had been too sudden and too extreme. She turned to find him watching her and regretted surrendering her jacket as she felt his eyes rest on the shadowed cleft between her breasts.

Taking in her heightened colour, his eyes narrowed in amusement, and he said, 'I like looking at you. You're a beautiful woman.' His eyes moved over her again, seeming to touch where they lingered on the partly revealed swell of flesh. 'I'm committing the picture to memory so that I can superimpose it over the office image tomorrow.'

She laughed suddenly, not so much at what he had said, but at the recollection of getting ready earlier. If he could have seen her washing her hair at the kitchen sink and checking her second-hand dress for mustiness, the last—or nearly the last—of his illusions would be destroyed.

'It's all makebelieve,' she told him. 'At midnight I change back.'

The glance he sent her was acute, though it was swiftly masked by a smile. Idly, he asked, 'What into?'

'Rags and tatters. What else?'

'I like the one better where the prince wakes the princess after a hundred years.' He smiled again, his eyes glimmering. She could see the pinpoint lights of the wall brackets reflected in them, then without warning, he demanded, 'How long have you been asleep, Lauren?'

She sat for a second in frozen stillness, then parried lightly, 'Are you casting yourself in the role of the handsome prince?'

'Yes,' he told her bluntly. 'And I know you hadn't been kissed in a hell of a long time, which there's got to be some reason for. It certainly isn't lack of opportunity. Nearly every man on the firm has shown himself willing and I've watched you give them all the brush-off. So what is it?'

She was saved by the waiter bringing them their drinks. He set them down on the table with a muted flourish, then the head waiter appeared with the menus. As he backed away, Warwick said under his breath, 'A pity. That's given you time to think.'

Without raising her eyes from the menu, Lauren said, 'My private life is private. I shouldn't tell you anything I didn't want to anyway.'

'But we'll see how far we can get. We'll start with the premise that there was an unfortunate experience with some man.'

'You don't need a degree in psychology to work that one out,' she said indifferently.

'And was he five feet eleven, with grey eyes and brown hair?'

Her startled eyes flew to his face. Numbly, she wondered how he could possibly know, then she remembered describing Trevor to him when he had asked what her fiancé was like. She had forgotten his staggering memory for minute detail.

He read the admission and nodded. 'We're making some progress. *Were* you engaged to him?'

'I'm not discussing it with you,' she said with flat finality.

Accepting it calmly, he abruptly changed the subject. 'Do you need any help with the menu?'

She nodded. 'My French isn't up to all of it. I never progressed beyond O level.'

In fact she was relieved to find how much of it she was familiar with. In her first job she had assisted in the preparations of endless dinner parties, and it amused her to think that her desperate plight had been a preparation for evenings like this. Some of the dishes, however, were specialities of the house and she could only guess at them. She pointed a questioning finger to them and Warwick leaned over. Like going over queries in the office, she thought, except that now she could feel the warmth of his thigh pressing against hers, and his breath lightly fanning her skin above the low neckline of her dress.

She prickled with an intense awareness and felt the fine hairs on her arms stand on end as he brushed against her. Deliberately she made her breathing even and tried to concentrate on the words before her, shaking her head at Warwick's suggestions. She wasn't fond of rich sauces, and to his mild exasperation she chose fresh asparagus and lamb cooked with herbs.

He moved away again when he had ordered. Half in the corner, he leaned back, watching her, the stem of his sherry glass slowly turning in his fingers. 'Should I be treading on your toes if I asked what you did before you came to Fenmore's?'

Lauren hesitated, but a reference from the Denholms was on her file and she suspected he would be familiar with it. Deciding she'd had enough of fencing, she said, 'You already know.'

He shrugged. 'Okay, we'll skip it. The real question is why does a poised, intelligent young woman take a job as a mother's help.'

'I had an interview before I was taken on at Fenmore's,' she reminded him acidly. He was going to go on probing and questioning, she knew, and to gain herself some respite she said, 'If you must know I didn't get on with my mother and I left home. At the time I had to get a job that provided living accommodation.'

His expression was unreadable and it was impossible to tell whether the explanation satisfied him or not. He asked, 'What about your father?'

'Divorced,' she replied briefly. Moving restlessly in her seat, she added, 'Do I get the same freedom to cross-examine you?'

'Ask away,' he invited.

'Very well. You're thirty-six. Why aren't you married?'

Laughing openly, he said, 'I laid a bet with myself that that would be the first question!'

'So you've won,' she returned, annoyed.

'But you were misinformed. I'm thirty-seven.'

He glanced sideways at her and she said coolly, 'You've probably had a birthday since I was told,' When he didn't speak she raised her brows at him. 'What's the matter? Isn't your life an open book either?'

'Not all of it,' he said easily, grinning at her. 'Some disclosures are governed by good taste, but in fact I was merely pondering. Do you want a flippant reply or a serious one?'

'Why ...' Taken aback for some reason, she stumbled over her words. 'Why, a serious one, I suppose.'

Warwick lit a cigarette and stared down at it, and she followed the direction of his gaze. He had well shaped hands, with fine, dark hairs on the backs of the long fingers. Unbidden, there came the memory of the way they had moved over her body when he was making love to her, and she felt a sudden heat rise in her and a return of that sharp, physical awareness. She tensed until it faded, thankful Warwick hadn't been watching her.

He looked up finally and said, 'Seriously then, I suppose it's an innate selfishness. I've always been perfectly satisfied with my life the way it is. Marriage involves considering the needs and wishes of someone else, and if I change my state I would have to be convinced that it was for the better.' He smiled faintly.

'And I don't make promises I feel I may not be able to keep, which is probably the real reason. The vows, as I recall them, are severely limiting. If I marry it will be in good faith.'

Sobered, she asked, 'Isn't it always?'

He cast her a derisive glance. 'Oh, come!—you must surely have some natural cynicism! Till death us do part is fairly freely interpreted!'

'I suppose so,' she admitted. 'Perhaps the marriage service should be rewritten to allow for genuine errors of judgement.'

'And perhaps people shouldn't embark on it quite so lightly.'

Hiding her surprise, she observed, 'Cautious. What would be your criterion, then?'

He leaned his head back against the wall, considering, and said at last, 'Whether this was the face I wanted to wake up and find beside me on the pillow in fifty years' time.'

'Fairly comprehensive.' A pang went through her at his words, so deep and unexpected that it stung her eyes. Terrified he might see, she summoned a smile as she said, 'At your age, don't you think you ought to make that forty years?'

'I'm healthy and ambitious,' he said, grinning lazily.

The charm was appearing now. Lauren had seen him switch it on with other people in the past, and to counteract it she deliberately recalled the memory of him as he had been at one period before, cold-faced and implacable. Had she loved him then? She wasn't sure. Even his own mother would have found it difficult. Somehow it was hard to imagine him with parents, and until he mentioned their dogs she hadn't even thought of it.

'What does that faraway expression signify?' he asked, recalling her.

She shook her head. 'Don't ask me why, but I was trying to imagine you with parents.'

He looked mildly surprised, then laughed. 'Well, I wasn't quarried, and there are three others besides me.'

'Which of your parents do you take after?'

'My mother. Her father was Italian,' he added, as Lauren's eyes slid up to his black head. 'And God only knows why anyone who spent the first twenty-two years of their life in Italy should settle on the name Warwick. Fortunately she's the only one who ever calls me by my full name, and then only when she thinks I've transgressed.'

'It could have been Stratford,' Lauren murmured. 'And what would you shorten that to?'

He winced and got to his feet as the head waiter appeared, soft-footed, to announce that their table was ready. Lauren slipped into the seat against the wall and Warwick said, 'A primitive human instinct.'

'What is?'

'To sit with one's back to the wall.'

She shook her head. 'You're searching too deeply. The truth is that I'm nosey and I like to look round the room.'

'Typical woman,' he commented. She smiled, beginning to feel lighthearted and relaxed, and was totally unprepared when he suddenly demanded, 'Why only Tuesdays and Thursdays?'

She swallowed, feeling the colour leave her face. She ought to have known that he would only wait for her guard to slip before attacking again.

Trying to keep her voice steady, she said, 'It's nothing sinister. My flatmate has a small daughter and I look after her in the evenings while Ann is at work. She serves in a pub and on Tuesdays and Thursdays she only does lunchtimes, so I'm free as long as I let her know in time. It was a condition when I moved in, and anyway I wouldn't let her down.'

Warwick didn't believe her, letting her see the scepticism in his probing glance before he slowly shook his head.

'Try again!'

'It's true,' Lauren insisted.

'Possibly, but not the whole truth and nothing but the truth. There's far more to it than that.'

'Why should you think that?'

Grimly impatient now, he said, 'Why? Because you're as taut as a piano wire, that's why!'

He leaned forward and prised her rigid fingers away from the glass in front of her. It held a single rose and she had been idly twirling it when he hit her with the question. She looked down at his hand still holding her fingers, and after a moment he released her and leaned back against his chair. 'Every time I mentioned working late or running you home you went into shock. The reason couldn't possibly be the one you've just given me—it's totally out of proportion and something you could easily have told me in the first place, so don't insult my intelligence.'

Laura nerved herself to look up at him and met his intent stare in a silence which seemed to go on for ever. Breaking it, he said slowly, 'You might as well tell me, because I shall find out.'

Dully, she said, 'Oh, leave me alone. Why can't you just accept that I work for you and I was completely happy with things the way they were?'

Warwick started to speak, but broke off as their first course arrived. The waiter was a burly Spaniard, and because of Lauren's position in the corner he was forced to lean over her to serve her asparagus. His black jacket smelled faintly of sweat, unmistakably male, and she pressed herself back hard against her chair until he had moved.

She wasn't even aware of having done it until she

caught Warwick's eye and saw the barely veiled triumph there.

Softly, he said, 'Last week you may have been completely happy. We both know that isn't true any more.'

It wasn't, but pride apart, she daren't let Warwick see how deeply he affected her. She began to eat her asparagus, wishing with all her heart that she was safely back home and this wasn't happening. It was stupid and futile to indulge her dreams. He could never be more than a lover. If it hadn't been for Mandy she knew she would have settled for that, with all its consequences, but Mandy needed a stable, balanced parent she could rely on, not the empty wreck Warwick would leave her at the end of an affair.

Her throat ached with the effort of control and she found the butter on the asparagus suddenly nauseating. Rinsing her fingers, she reached for her wine and looked up to find Warwick watching her narrowly. Indicating her plate, he asked, 'Is there anything wrong with it?'

'No, it's fine. The butter was a bit sickly, that's all.' She smiled slightly. 'I have fairly simple tastes. I'm afraid all this is wasted on me.'

Still with that curiously assessing gaze, he said, 'You're totally unimpressed by it, aren't you?'

'Why, I . . .' She faltered to a halt. 'You're forcing me to sound ungracious.'

His brows lifted in mock surprise. 'You've become very polite all of a sudden. Earlier in the evening you didn't hesitate to tell me you were only coming under duress.' He swallowed the rest of his wine, absently blotting the condensation from his fingers with the napkin before he spoke again. 'Though I can't really complain. You've made it obvious enough that I don't impress you in any way. What is your standard, I wonder?'

Lauren hesitated, and with reluctant honesty said, 'I have a great deal of respect for your business ability.'

That at least was completely true. He had a lightning brain and the type of mind which could assess a problem instantly. Many a time as well she had ploughed through a mountain of figures with a calculator to find the total was only a few pounds out from his casual approximation. Warwick was undoubtedly from a comfortable background, but he wasn't living on inherited wealth. Fenmore's had been a small firm when he took it over and he had built it up by his own flair and ability and single-minded effort.

Bleakly, he said, 'Don't go overboard with the accolades. What you really mean is that I don't affect you as a man.'

Caught on a hook, she wondered helplessly what she could say. If she agreed with him, in what sort of light did that put her complete capitulation in his apartment? In effect she would be telling him that if enough champagne was poured into her she would be willing to go to bed with any man.

To answer him was humiliation either way, and she had to force the words out when she said at last, 'You know that isn't so.'

She couldn't look at him as she spoke and for a moment she wondered if he had heard, then half under his breath he muttered, 'God, I thought I'd never get you to say it! And even then I had to push you into a corner where you either had to admit it or make yourself look cheap.'

Too late she saw the trap he had manoeuvred her into, and she felt anger rise in her, both with him and for herself for her lack of perception. She stared at him, and he said, 'No, you haven't told me anything I didn't already know, but I wanted to make you say it to me.'

'Why?' she asked, through stiff lips. 'To pander to your ego?'

'Don't be ridiculous,' he told her brusquely.

'Then what was your reason?'

He leaned forward, holding her with dark, intent eyes. 'I told you before there's been something between us for a long time now. I want to find what it is without you fighting me every step of the way.'

Her voice tight, Lauren said, 'Take my word for it, you're wasting your time.'

She reached blindly for her glass, but Warwick put his hand over hers before she could lift it.

'Leave it until you've had something else to eat,' he ordered. 'From what I've seen of you, one sherry and one glass of wine on an empty stomach is practically enough to put you out. You must have the weakest head for alcohol I've ever struck!'

She smiled at him, waveringly and without humour. 'I have. I think I'll give it up before it leads me into any more—uncontrolled—situations.'

Stiffening, he returned, 'Whether you believe me or not, I had every intention of taking you straight home from that dinner.'

Remembering his irritability and barely controlled temper, Lauren did believe him. She was silent for a moment, then she asked quietly, 'Why *did* you offer to take me?'

His expression hardened, forming his lips into a straight line. 'I couldn't watch out for you all the time, and you might just have been fool enough to go with Richardson.' A harsh note invaded his voice. 'And no bloody salesman was going to get what I wanted!'

CHAPTER SIX

When Warwick drew up outside the flat he made no move to switch the engine off, saying fatalistically, 'I presume I don't get invited in.'

Lauren hesitated. Perhaps it was playing with fire, but Mandy and Sarah slept at the back of the house. They were used to the sounds of the comings and goings of the other tenants, and like traffic noise it had ceased to impinge on their awareness. Once they were settled they seldom woke for anything except illness.

Making up her mind, she said, 'You can come in if you like, but I can only offer you coffee.'

His head turned quickly. She knew he was puzzled, though it was too dark to read any expression. Ambiguously, he said, 'I wasn't expecting anything else,' and she was uncertain whether to be annoyed or reassured as she led the way in.

Obvious film music from the television penetrated the hall, and Lauren left Warwick standing in the dim light while she checked that Ann wasn't watching in her nightdress. When it was a film which finished late she often undressed first, but fortunately on this occasion she had taken off no more than her shoes. She looked up with an enquiring smile as Lauren put her head round the door, the expression changing to startled incredulity when Lauren asked, 'Are you fit for company?'

Mouthing, 'Warwick?' Ann uncurled herself rapidly from the chair and thrust her feet back into her sandals so that she was her usual picture of tall elegance when Warwick walked in.

Watching her face for her reactions, Lauren saw the almost universal one in women confronted by Warwick for the first time. He hit them like a blow. Ann was no exception, but her response was unwilling. As she turned back to Lauren her eyes clearly asked what she could be thinking of to bring him in.

Lauren's thoughts echoed the unspoken question. She wondered what sudden madness had made her allow him into this separate life which had been safe from him before. His expensive, immaculate clothes made their pleasant little room seem shabby, like the new suite she had bought which showed up the faded carpet. This evening, garbed by Sheila Denholm's faultless taste, she had been his equal, but his presence now demonstrated their differences plainly. She didn't belong in his world. Unmarried, with a six-year-old daughter, she didn't belong in anyone's, but before it had been something she could accept without too much regret.

Ann moved towards the television and Warwick said, 'Don't switch it off because of me.'

She made a small, dismissing gesture. 'I wasn't so much watching it as sunk in apathy. Shall I make us all some coffee? I could do with a cup even if no one else could.'

Her indifferent manner bordered on rudeness, and when she had gone to the kitchen Warwick raised his brows. 'Was she waiting up to make sure you got safely home?'

Uncomfortable that Warwick should know she had been discussing him, Lauren felt the colour tinge her cheeks and said stiffly, 'I share a bedroom with her. She couldn't help knowing I was out all night.'

'But presumably she also knows you were returned unravished?'

Lauren shrugged. 'Perhaps she still thinks you have designs on me in spite of that.'

'She's perfectly right, but since the same would apply to the majority of men, why am I singled out for disfavour?'

When she didn't reply, he said, 'Or have you just formed yourself into a little ménage of man-haters? Since there's been no mention of a husband, I gather she's divorced or separated.'

'She could be unmarried,' Lauren pointed out, driven by a recklessness which terrified her the moment the words were out. God, what had possessed her? She felt her mouth go dry as Warwick looked at her curiously.

'Statistically, it's the least likely, and I didn't want to be accused of maligning her.' He paused. 'Why? Is she?'

'No.' She got up quickly with the excuse of fetching him an ashtray. As she placed it in front of him she said, 'She's separated. She hasn't got round to divorcing him yet.'

Warwick lit a cigarette, watching her from under heavy lids. 'Why did you say she could be unmarried?'

With difficulty Lauren prevented herself from swallowing, knowing the action would be revealing. 'Oh, just something you once said,' she told him, making her voice composed.

'Remind me.'

Her ears picked up the sound of crockery rattling in the kitchen and she wished desperately that Ann would come back in to save her. 'It was a long time ago, when Janice in the pool found she was pregnant.'

'Yes, I remember.' He waited a second, then prompted, 'So?'

'It wasn't anything particular that you said, but your tone seemed to imply condemnation.'

'Very probably. It's my opinion that promiscuous eighteen-year-olds should be more careful.'

Suddenly angry, Lauren said sharply, 'The old

double standard! It's perfectly all right for a man, but a girl is labelled promiscuous!'

Mildly, he said, 'It was only her carelessness that I was criticising. Don't hold me responsible for general opinion.'

'You sounded as though you subscribed to it.'

'Perhaps to some extent,' he admitted. 'Unfair, I agree, but it's an unfair world, and a man's point of view may be slightly different. If I marry I want reasonable certainty that any children I'm bringing up and educating are really mine, and that it won't be the bank manager's son who inherits what I've worked to build up. Rightly or wrongly, the odds seem less favourable in the case of a girl like Janice.' He studied Lauren's face for a moment, and half impatiently, went on, 'Anyway, why this sudden defence of a girl whose lifestyle you obviously disagree with?'

'I don't really know.' She wound a piece of hair round her finger in an unthinkingly nervous gesture. 'Perhaps my sense of justice was offended by you calling her promiscuous.'

'The dictionary definition of the word is indiscriminate or casual. I used it in its dictionary sense, because I've received a couple of very clear invitations from her myself.' Lauren looked up quickly and he gave her a sardonic grin. 'I can recognise an unspoken offer as easily as an unspoken brush-off.'

She flushed. 'And taken advantage of them, no doubt.'

'On occasions, though not in this instance.'

'Don't you think that's hypocrisy?'

'No,' he said, unperturbed. 'I've never pretended to be anything other than what I am.'

So now she knew, Lauren thought. To the chairman of Fenmore's, women were still divided into those you married and those you didn't.

Interrupting her thoughts, Ann shouldered the door open, the mugs clinking on the tray. With sinking heart, Lauren saw that perversity had made her use the kitchen mugs, deliberately underlining the gulf Warwick was already aware of. Lauren had seen his eyes wander round the room, lingering briefly on the heap of toys in the corner, but he hadn't bothered to make any trite, insincere remarks about how cosy or comfortable it was. His own apartment, like his office, was furnished with spare, uncluttered luxury because that was how he liked it.

While they were drinking their coffee Ann made an attempt to cover her hostility with polite small talk, but after she had made her excuses and gone to bed, Warwick said, an edge to his voice, 'Tell her the scenario with the lord of the manor and the honest housemaid is outdated. These days he'd be taken to tribunal for sexual harassment!'

'Tell her yourself,' Lauren retorted. She held his gaze steadily for a moment. 'Because she's not entirely wrong, is she?'

There was a long pause, then Warwick said evenly, 'I think I'd like you to elaborate on that.'

'You used the fact that I work for you to make me come out with you tonight. You knew you weren't giving me much choice.'

'Possibly,' he admitted at last.

She sent him a scornful glance and began to gather the mugs back on to the tray. As she passed him to get back to her own chair, he reached out swiftly, catching her wrist to pull her down on him. She struggled even though she knew it was futile, and holding her against his chest, he muttered, 'Stop panicking! What do you think I can do to you with your chaperone next door?' When she quietened he released her wrist and encircled her with his arms, loosely, but with his hands clasped to prevent her escape. 'All right, so I did use the fact that you work for me. Not very admirable means, but you force me into them.'

Rigid in his embrace, Lauren said despairingly, 'Warwick, I'm not just playing hard to get.'

'I know.' He gave a short laugh. 'You've been too emphatic for that.'

'Then why won't you give up? I've told you you're wasting your time.'

He slid his hand up to the betraying pulse in the side of her neck and held it there so that the throbbing seemed intensified. 'Because what you say and what you feel are two different things.'

Jerking her head away from his touch, she said sharply, 'Your vast experience again!' For a moment she prised uselessly at his fingers, then sighed. 'Let me go, Warwick. At least believe me when I say I'm not going to be the latest on your list.'

'I'll believe you, but in return, stop basing your opinions on those of Meg and the typing pool. You've got a brain and five senses of your own.'

'Their opinions aren't all hearsay,' she retorted. 'Myra Hamilton seems to have been a first-hand witness.'

'Yes,' he said, suddenly savage. 'She was a mistake I'm not going to be allowed to forget.' He took a deep breath and said more calmly, 'She's already done all the talking herself, so I'm not giving away any secrets. I took what she offered. For a while it suited us both, but then she began to get more ambitious ideas, so I ended it.'

'And had to get yourself another secretary,' said Lauren in flat tones. 'Thank you, but I'd rather history didn't repeat itself. If I'm going to learn from experience I prefer it to be someone else's rather than mine.'

'Oh, for God's sake!' he exclaimed with raw impatience. 'Myra was different! It was purely sexual on both sides. We went to bed together, but otherwise she felt no more for me than I did for her. And she left Fenmore's of her own accord because she'd dug a pit for herself with her tongue!'

Which would be true enough, Lauren conceded. But even if Myra hadn't talked so freely? She shuddered inwardly, appalled at the thought of ever finding herself in the same position.

She stirred and turned to meet Warwick's narrowed eyes. 'All right, perhaps Myra was different, but ...' She raised her shoulders helplessly. 'I can't somehow see you being content with merely taking me out.'

'No,' he agreed. 'It's the way I am—the way I'm made, but I don't only want to make love to you—can I get that into your head?' He sighed with a harsh sound. 'When I ask you to come out with me it's because I want to be with you. Where's the harm for you in that?'

None that he would be able to see, Lauren thought, but his question made no allowance for emotions— stupid dreams of being the face on the other pillow when physical needs were quieter and less urgent.

Summoning all her inner reserves, she said, 'There's no point in all this. If we go on for ever, we're still going to come back to the same thing. That night in your apartment was a mistake—something I wish had never happened and which won't happen again. I'm your secretary and that's the way I want to stay. If you won't accept that, I shall have to leave.'

Warwick stared at her, irritable and angry with frustration, then muttered, 'Hell, there's only one way to stop you talking drivel!'

Still holding her, he twisted round so that she was thrown down against the cushions, her arms pinned to her sides. It was impossible to evade his descending lips, but she opposed him with a fierce resistance. His response was to kiss her harder until pain forced her to give way and allow him the warmth of her mouth.

For a while she tried to concentrate on discomforts—her smarting lip, one of her legs twisted awkwardly beneath the weight of his, a few strands of hair caught on something and tugging sharply. But the sensations faded, overridden by stronger ones, until the entire area of her consciousness was centred on his ever deepening kiss and the strong surge of desire it aroused within her. When he lifted his head she drew a quick, ragged breath, her eyes still closed to limit the world to the feel of his body pressing her against the cushions, and the drugging, male scent of his skin.

Quietly, he said, 'Now tell me you only want to be my secretary.'

If there had been triumph in his voice she would have reacted with anger, but though she knew he had set out to prove a point he wasn't taunting her with it, and she pulled his head down beside hers in wordless acknowledgement. He turned his lips to her throat and ran the tips of his fingers up her arm, stirring the almost invisible hairs, then trailed them round her neck and the hollow beneath her ear. His touch was sensual but without urgency, finely judged to give pleasure but not alarm, and lying quietly, Lauren felt the wild turbulence in her veins settle back into a more even rhythm.

Warwick blew lightly into her ear, then suddenly propped himself on his elbow to look at her. 'Get Ann to arrange a baby-sitter for Friday.'

Immediately she stiffened, the spell broken. 'No!'

She waited for his quick, impatient frown, but as though they had never spoken he resumed his delicate tracery round her shoulder, then lowered his lips to her throat. His tongue was unexpectedly hot on her skin and she gave a tiny jerk in a reaction she could not control, then he slid his mouth down to the valley between her breasts.

A vivid memory, as arousing as his touch, flooded through her. Murmuring, 'No,' she tried to push him away, but he held her arms with a quiet strength, then slowly and deliberately pulled her dress and the straps of her bra down over her shoulders. The crossover bodice parted, revealing her breasts, and she felt his gaze like a tangible touch as he stared down at them before raising his eyes to her face. Protest died as she stared back, held still by his regard as surely as by physical restraint. Then in the silence she heard the click of the light switch from the bedroom next door and the sound of the wardrobe door being noisily banged.

The trancelike immobility snapped and she tried to sit up. 'Ann . . .'

'She won't walk in on us without warning,' Warwick told her with calm conviction. 'That was for my benefit—to remind me that she's here.'

He was right, Lauren knew, but the intrusive moment had brought her back to earth. Now she was only conscious of being half naked under Warwick's gaze, and she felt herself colour as she tried to cover herself. His hands stayed her, pushing her back against the cushions as he silenced her partially uttered objections with his mouth, his lips moving and probing until she was submissive again.

He drew away from her then, opening a space between them so that he could bring his hands down to cup the swell of her breasts. The light, feathering touch of his thumbs, experienced and erotic, made her catch her breath. A novice against an expert, she knew she was succumbing and she tried to wrench herself back from the road he was leading her down, frightened because it was what she wanted herself and he was loosening her grip on sanity.

She gripped his wrists, and at once his hands were stilled and he looked down at her searchingly. The desire revealed in her darkened eyes was overlaid with fear, and reading her expression Warwick shook his head.

'No, I wasn't going to—not here. Making love with one ear stretched for interruptions isn't the ideal. I intended no more than this.' His hands tightened briefly and resumed their caress, then his thumbs slid aside and he lowered his head. In the moment before his mouth touched, he murmured, 'And this.'

Lauren quivered, the inner hunger intensifying to an ache that almost made her forget Ann's presence in the next room. Then panic flared again, making her suddenly rigid, and Warwick transferred his lips to her throat.

'Gently, gently—I told you I know what I'm doing. I won't take it any further.'

Her continued tension conveyed her doubt and he swung his feet to the floor and sat up. One hand on her throat, he held it lightly between finger and thumb. 'Yes, I know I said so once before, but on that occasion I was—thrown a little off balance by the unexpected.' He trailed his fingers down her neck, then abruptly pulled her dress back into position. 'This time circumstances decree that I should be rationed to half a loaf.'

Standing as he spoke, he smiled faintly and reached out to touch her cheek in a gesture he might have made to a child. 'To be honest, I don't believe for a moment that your friend would come back in, but while I might be willing to run the risk of being caught *in flagrante delicto*, it could rather take the edge off the experience for you.'

He turned away from her again and picked up his jacket, feeling in the pocket for his cigarettes. Lauren watched as he lit one, his dark head tilted sideways, eyes narrowed against the flame. Strange that she had known him for so long, yet this was only the third time she had seen him without the jacket and waistcoat he always wore in the air-conditioned atmosphere of the office. Her pulse quickened as her glance took in the powerful sweep of his shoulders, narrowing down to the low hips and flat stomach. He was a big man, large-framed, and she remembered how his size had always increased her fear of him in the past.

He raised his eyes quickly from the flame of the lighter, and caught watching him, she flushed. He was too astute and she knew he had registered her momentarily unguarded expression. But then he had just told her, even if not in so many words, that she would have let him seduce her if he had brought all his persuasion to bear.

She was still lying half propped up on the arm of the settee and he came and sat down again, his back against the curve of her stomach and upper thighs. Looking at her quizzically, he said, 'So tell Ann to get a baby-sitter for Friday.'

'This time I'll ask,' she said. 'Why?'

'Because I'm taking you to a dinner. Semi-business.'

She wondered if he was serious, and asked, 'Why would you want me at a semi-business dinner?'

'For protection,' he told her, a thread of amusement appearing in his voice.

'You must be the last man in the world who needs protecting,' she said uncertainly.

'Generally yes, but in this case I don't want to be forced into publicly—defending myself.' He met her questioning glance and said, 'My brother-in-law is trying to set up a deal under the usual polite cover of an invitation to stay for a few days for a couple of rounds of golf and a bit of sailing and that sort of thing.'

'Then your sister is giving the dinner?'

Wild implications flew round her startled brain, but she must have successfully hidden her astonishment, because he merely said, 'Yes.'

He put out his cigarette, carefully aligning the square ash tray with the edge of the table. The action was somehow uncharacteristic, lacking his customary decisiveness, and he suddenly pushed it away and looked back at her.

'Are you involved in the deal?' Lauren asked.

He nodded. 'Which is where it might get awkward. The man we're negotiating with is a widower and he's bringing his daughter. We were all fairly friendly at one time when I lived down there, and I have a faint presentiment that Tessa might try to revive the good old days over Rachel's dinner table. She's recently divorced her husband.'

How friendly was friendly? Lauren wondered. Flippantly, she suggested, 'Take Vivian. She'd be delighted to look after you.'

'I daresay, but I should be lucky to get a card from Rachel at Christmas if I did,' he said drily. 'And Vivian would hardly fill the bill. Tessa would realise straight away that she was only a—temporary liaison.'

Keeping her voice light, Lauren returned, 'For heaven's sake, you must surely know one or two women who *are* respectable! Or is all this a front for the fact that you want someone to take notes?'

'No, just to look beautiful and co-operate in convincing Tessa that I'm already tied up.' He paused, then said, 'Rachel would expect us to stay overnight.' He caught the swift change in her expression and added, 'No, it wouldn't be what you suspect. The serious talking is likely to be after everyone else had gone to bed—it usually is, and though Rachel doesn't care what I do elsewhere, she would be less tolerant in her own home.'

'What sort of thing would I wear?' Lauren asked. She realised she was committing herself, and went on hurriedly, 'If I came.'

'Long but not too formal. The cream one you wore last week would be ideal.'

She nodded, hoping the hem hadn't been marked, because her wardrobe didn't contain anything else even remotely suitable. She wanted to go, but she recognised that she was seizing on the fact that Warwick said it was business as an excuse, so she said, 'I'll let you know one way or the other when I've spoken to Ann.'

'All right.' Sensing that the battle was already more than halfway won, he made no attempt to pressure her, and glancing at his watch he got to his feet. 'You've just changed back, Cinderella.'

She looked at him blankly and he held his watch for her to see. 'Midnight.'

'Oh,' she said, remembering. Somehow the conversation at the start of the evening seemed a long way away. She looked round for her sandals, but Warwick reached down and pulled her to her feet, running the palms of his hands slowly from her shoulders to her elbows before drawing her against him. He kissed her gently, then with an urgent passion that roused a swift surge of desire in her. For the first time she responded in the same way, tentatively and half fearfully exploring his mouth in return, and she felt the muscles in his back contract sharply under her fingers as he suddenly strained her to him. The message of his body was basic and unmistakable, and when she made no attempt to draw away he lifted his head and muttered thickly against her mouth, 'Don't make promises you're not prepared to keep.'

She did move away then and he looked down at her, his lips twisted into something that was not quite a smile. 'Second thoughts? Or perhaps you weren't thinking at all.'

Still shaken by the explosion of feeling, Lauren didn't—couldn't reply, and he picked up his jacket by the loop and slung it over his shoulder, pausing by the front door to glance back and say ironically, 'Sweet dreams!'

As Lauren watched him go down the path and swing himself into the low car, illogically, her only thought was that she hadn't thanked him for the meal. She laughed silently to herself. How ridiculous could you get, to be concerned with manners at such a time?

She found her hands were still shaking as she went through her nightly routine of removing her make-up. What remained of it, anyway. In the mirror the last vestiges of lipstick were gone, and she slowly traced her finger round the swollen curves of her mouth, wondering if it would still show tomorrow. It was embarrassingly obvious now and she hoped Ann was asleep as she quietly opened the bedroom door.

She was reading by the bedside lamp, but she leaned over and switched on the main light, studying Lauren for a moment before commenting, 'Thorough.'

When Lauren made no reply, she closed the book and dropped it on to the bed. 'Look, I'm sorry about earlier on. I've been lying here thinking about it, and if I can't sort myself out I shouldn't be telling anyone else what to do. If you love him you love him, so ignore me and do what comes naturally.'

'If you're asking me, I didn't,' said Lauren. She slipped out of her dress and sat at the dressing table to clear the tangles from her hair. Putting the brush down with a slight clatter, she said, 'He wants me to go to a dinner party his sister is giving on Friday.'

Through the mirror she saw Ann's grey eyes narrow in speculation as she said slowly, 'Then I'll break the new rule I've just made for myself. You've *got* to tell him about Mandy.'

'It isn't as momentous as it sounds. His brother-in-law is trying to swing a deal with a man they've got staying with them. His daughter is there too and Warwick wants to use me as a shield. He doesn't want to offend them.'

'The poor helpless male,' Ann jeered. 'He could always scream rape!' She grimaced and said, 'Sorry,' before adding, 'but if he's involving you with relatives you've got to tell him.'

'I know.' With an abrupt movement Lauren turned on the stool to face her. 'I will. After Friday.'

'No, you won't,' Ann said relentlessly. 'You'll keep finding another excuse to put it off. For God's sake get it over with.'

'Just this one more time,' Lauren said pleadingly.

She lay for a long while thinking after they had finally put out the light, coming reluctantly awake when Mandy bounced on the end of her bed just before seven. Tiredly she wondered why children insisted on being so exuberantly alive during the holidays when there was no need for them to get up too early.

After supervising Mandy's washing, she held on to her patience while she tied her shoelaces. Tongue between her teeth, Mandy breathed heavily until it was accomplished, then skipped out to sit on the bottom stair and wish all the tenants good morning as they came down for their newspapers and mail. She liked to see if she could read the names on the letters and put them in separate piles on the hall table, and she came back presently complaining, 'Grown-ups' writing is *terrible*!'

'Mine isn't,' Lauren told her, setting the milk and breakfast bowls on the table. 'Go and ask Sarah what she wants for breakfast, there's a good girl.'

She looked up when Mandy made no move. She was standing by the kitchen door, biting her lip uncertainly, and she suddenly broke out, 'You went out with a man in a grey car last night.'

Lauren paused, then reached the cereals down from the cupboard. 'Yes,' she said, keeping her voice level. 'How did you know that?'

'Mrs Walker told me just now when she came for her letter,' Mandy supplied. 'She said it was a nice car and she asked me who he was.'

She would, Lauren thought bitterly. She spent so much time looking round her net curtains it was a wonder she ever got anything done. Mandy was crying again, not the angry, defiant sobbing of yesterday, but frightened tears, somehow imploring. 'I don't want you to go out in a car with a man!'

'Come here,' said Lauren, sitting down. She held out her arms and Mandy threw herself into them. 'Now tell me what this is all about.' She rested her chin for a moment on the smooth red hair, then looked down into Mandy's face. 'You like to go and play with your friends, don't you? When you went to Simon's party last week, did I cry and say I didn't want you to go?'

Mandy shook her head, sniffing, and Lauren fished a tissue out of her pocket and wiped her nose. 'So why should you cry if I go out occasionally?'

'I just don't want you to go,' Mandy said, muffled against her housecoat. There was genuine fear in the tense little body, but Lauren couldn't get her to say more. She soothed her as much as she could, but Mandy dogged her every footstep until she left to catch her bus, and Lauren's last view was of her small, strained face at the window as she waved goodbye.

What strange, unimagined things went on in children's minds? she wondered. And how could you reassure them if you couldn't find out? By the time she got to work she was even more divided about going to the dinner. Mandy's upset this time was very real— quite different from the previous night, and Lauren could foresee trouble if it wasn't sorted out before Friday.

When Warwick came in she tried to hide her mental upheaval, smoothing the frown from her face before she turned to greet him, but he checked in his stride as he came towards her, his narrowed eyes measuring. She summoned a smile, but his expression did not relax, and he halted by her chair and ordered curtly, 'Don't start again. You're coming.'

Now was the time to say no, but the familiar helplessness invaded her when he reached out to touch her bruised lip with reflective gentleness before saying, 'So no more arguments.'

He was gone before she could make any protest. From his office she heard the ritual sounds as he unlatched his briefcase and opened it on his desk, rustling the papers as he put them in order before ringing down to Meg for a string of calls.

So much for free will and resolution! Lauren thought wryly, but worry fretted her half the morning until Meg rang through to say there was a personal call for her. 'Phone box,' she added shortly, and Lauren's hand tightened on the receiver. Only Ann ever rang her, so it had to be to do with Mandy. Her mind went back to the disquieting scene that morning, and it seemed an age before the click of the connection and Ann's brisk, 'Hello?'

'What is it?' Lauren asked sharply. She knew Warwick could hear her through the open door, but in her anxiety she didn't care.

'No problem,' Ann assured her, her voice airy, and Lauren slumped back in her chair. 'I rang because of that bit of trouble you had this morning. In case you were worried about making arrangements, I thought I'd let you know I've fixed it and you can relax.'

'You're sure?' Lauren queried. She would have liked more than just that cryptic encouragement, but the faint echo on the line warned her that Meg was listening in.

'Positive. You can go ahead.'

'Thanks,' said Lauren. And see what you can make of that, she silently added to Meg as she put the receiver back. She returned to her typing, wondering if she would ever rid herself of the conviction that personal calls meant disaster. As she turned her head to read her shorthand she saw Warwick standing in the doorway, drawn out no doubt by that note of panic in her first question.

She let out her breath in relief when he disappeared again without comment. After Friday, she vowed. Definitely I'll tell him about Mandy after Friday.

With a jolt she realised that unless she postponed it for another fortnight she would have very little opportunity, because she wasn't at work the following week. She and Mandy were going to a caravan by the sea, their first real holiday together, and she had opted to take the rest of her holiday beforehand so that she could prepare for it at leisure.

She felt a sudden chill as she wondered if this time next week she would still be working at Fenmore's. Her fingers slowed on the keys and she realised she was staring into space and Warwick had come back in and was regarding her enquiringly. She caught his eye and said, half apologetically, 'I was thinking ahead. Ann's just rung to say she's made arrangements for her little girl on Friday.'

He said, 'Good,' but there was still enquiry in his gaze as it rested on her, and to forestall any questions she reminded him hurriedly, 'You've got an appointment in ten minutes. I've put the figures you'll need in your folder.'

He nodded his thanks and went back to his office, and neither of them made any further reference to the dinner for the rest of the day.

Lauren found it was odd and uncomfortable taking his dictation with the memory of the previous evening between them. There was a total switch in Warwick's personality when he was at work. Hearing his sometimes sharp commands on the phone, the impatience in his voice if someone was slow to carry out an order, she found it hard to believe this was the man who had made love to her. In front of others he still called her Miss Peters, and he carried out his own work with the same fast efficiency. It was almost business as usual, except that every so often she would catch his eyes on her and knew he was remembering just as she was.

She was impatient to get home that night to discover the meaning behind Ann's carefully worded message. She was in the bedroom, wildly thrusting the contents of a drawer from side to side, and she greeted Lauren with relief. 'Thank God! Have you got a spare pair of tights? I've put my damned fingernail through my only decent pair and the shops shut in five minutes!'

'I've got a new pair you can have,' Lauren reassured her. Ann relaxed on to the bed and she said, 'I daren't ask you any more when you rang me. How have you fixed it?'

Ann looked smug. 'Pure brilliance. My mother was asking not long ago if they could have Sarah to stay for the weekend some time, so I've arranged for them both to go, Friday morning till Sunday night. You can go off with a clear conscience. Mandy won't know a thing about it.'

'Oh, no!' Lauren exclaimed. 'It's an imposition!'

'Of course it isn't. It will be far less trouble with both of them. One child you have to amuse and it gets wearing. When there are two of them you only have to stop them quarrelling. Hell, they're *my* parents! Would I suggest it if I thought I was doing them a bad turn?'

'No,' Lauren agreed. 'Thanks, Ann, that's marvellous.'

'I thought it was as well, and if you really want to thank me, find me those tights!'

Lauren grinned and got them out of her drawer, and Ann said, 'There's a letter for you, by the way. It came second post.'

From Trevor's mother, Lauren thought without enthusiasm. They kept up an infrequent correspondence, prompted on both sides by a vague sense of duty. Neither of them wrote more than two or three times a year normally, and she scanned through it quickly, searching for the explanation for an unusually speedy reply to her own letter.

Mrs Munro always preserved the ritual of enquiring after their health and giving trivial bits of news before she embarked on the main point. Eventually Lauren found it at the bottom of the second page. Trevor had got married last week. It was very sudden and they hadn't known anything about it until afterwards. He was coming out of the Navy and he and his wife were going to live in Scotland where he had managed to find a job.

Lauren read the passage through again. The information was awkwardly phrased as though Mrs Munro had spent too long in thinking about it before she committed it to paper. She was obviously uncomfortable about imparting the news, and Lauren wondered if Trevor's hastily acquired bride was also pregnant. It was a matter of complete indifference anyway. Feeling totally detached, she read on, detecting agitation in the next part. Trevor's wife knew nothing about Mandy, and since they would be living so far away, Mrs Munro felt it was best if she was never told.

What does she think I might do? Lauren wondered. Suddenly serve a paternity order on him after all this time? Impatiently she folded the letter and put it back in her bag. There was a hint in the general tone that Mrs Munro would be relieved if this last contact between them were to cease, and she was in wholehearted agreement. It was a link with the past better severed.

But though Trevor's marriage meant nothing to her she felt faintly uneasy. Trying to analyse her feelings, she could think of no logical reason. It was simply that she was somehow convinced that outside influences beyond her control were impelling her towards changes she neither planned nor desired.

CHAPTER SEVEN

By Friday, Mandy was wildly excited at the prospect of sleeping away from home. Lauren wished her own anticipation could be as unmixed. She veered between the total conviction that she should never have agreed to it, and an excitement almost as intense as Mandy's. Uppermost, though, was the foreboding that she was making things more difficult for herself. Basically, she knew she should obey her instincts and back out from it, and she was excusing her own weakness with the pretext that it was too late now all the arrangements had been made.

At work, Warwick skimmed through the post in her tray, then tossed it back and commented, 'There's nothing to keep us among that lot. We'll call it a day at lunchtime and I'll take you home.'

Without looking up, Lauren felt his eyes on her, ready to gauge her slightest reaction. Secure in the knowledge that Mandy would be gone before then, her face showed an undisturbed calm, and after a pause he said, 'I'd like to start about five if that's all right with you. The traffic will be heavy going out and it will take us some time.'

She'd intended to buy a new pair of shoes in her lunch hour, but she could just as easily get them nearer home, so she said, 'Fine.'

She knew Warwick was speculating on her unworried agreement and pushed back the ever-present stirrings of guilt. It was *her* life, not his, that was being upset. Neither her past nor her future were any concern of his. If he had only taken her straight home from that

farewell dinner . . . She stifled her thoughts. Too many
of them nowadays began 'if only' . . .

The shoes proved unexpectedly difficult. Eventually
she managed to find an elegant pair of gold sandals that
was within her price range, but the prolonged search
made her late and she still had to put her overnight
things in a case when Warwick arrived.

He was early, so it wasn't really her fault, but she
found herself apologising as she took him into the front
room to wait. She was nervous, absurdly aware of him
in his casual, fine-knit sweater and fawn slacks. The
contrast to his usual dark, conservative suits seemed to
emphasise the change in their relationship, and the
evening ahead suddenly took on a much greater
magnitude.

She went into the bedroom and quickly packed her
necessities, then paused in front of the long dress,
wondering if it would be better loose in the back of the
car. Warwick might have things of his own on the seat,
and she turned to go and ask him, then gave a startled
gasp as she met him in the doorway.

He was frowning heavily as his eyes ranged round the
ceiling, taking in the evidence of damp, and he said
abruptly, 'God, do you sleep in here?'

'I presume that was a rhetorical question,' Lauren
returned, picking up her small case. She draped the
dress over her arm and moved towards the door,
making it obvious she was ready to leave. Ignoring her,
he prowled round the room examining the electrical
sockets, and finally stood on the end of her bed to
unscrew the aged ceiling rose above the light. His lips
were compressed as he got down and dusted his fingers
together, and with suppressed rage in his voice he said,
'The wiring in this place is bloody lethal! All this stuff
was obsolete thirty years ago!'

Lauren already knew. The electrician they had called

in to renew a switch plate had told them as much, and she said wryly, 'The fuse board down in the cellar is terrifyingly familiar to all of us, but you soon learn which combination of appliances is likely to black you out.'

Grimly, he said, 'Thank your stars the fuses do blow. Who's your landlord?'

'He won't do anything,' Lauren told him. 'We've all tried, separately and together. If it's anything he doesn't want to know he simply doesn't answer the letter.'

'With all due respect to your efforts, I don't think he'd ignore a letter from me.'

His smile held menace, and disturbed, Lauren said quickly, 'No, please don't. Ann is the official tenant and I don't want to make things unpleasant for her. The landlord knows he'd have queues of people perfectly willing to take it as it is.'

For a moment she thought Warwick was going to argue, then he grimaced round. 'Are you really so keen to stay here? I could find you somewhere better than this.'

'No, thank you,' Lauren said shortly.

He thrust his hands into the pockets of his slacks and looked down at her, his brows a solid line.

'Don't leap to conclusions. I wasn't offering to set you up.' Her colour rose, and seeing it he relented. 'All right, perhaps it was a natural presumption—I admit I've done it in the past. But in this case it was a straight offer of help. I can pull strings you wouldn't even dream of.' He looked round again. 'You must have another bedroom that the child sleeps in. Is it as bad as this?'

Lauren had a swift upsurge of fright in case he decided to go and investigate the other room. If he did he would see the twin beds, each with a favourite toy adorning the cover, and all the other evidence that the room had two occupants. She fought the feeling back, seeing Warwick go still, his eyes watchful and astute. Hurriedly, she said, 'The sockets are the same everywhere, but this is the only room that's damp.'

As though she hadn't spoken he continued to hold her with that alert gaze. 'What did I say then to throw you into a panic?'

'Nothing,' she said, with forced lightness. Rationality returned and she realised that whatever he suspected about her it would be nowhere near the truth. Glancing at her watch, she reminded him, 'You said you wanted to start at five.'

He didn't move, his eyes still searching her face. The silence stretched, and he said finally, 'Tell me.'

His voice was gentle but she sensed that he was using all the power of his will to make her answer him. For a moment it swamped her, then she dragged herself free and shook her head.

He reached out and pressed the flat of his thumb against her chin, tipping her head back. 'Because you think it will alter my opinion of you?'

'I don't really know what your opinion is anyway.' She could feel his probing stare, but she refused to meet it and twisted her head away. In sharp, defensive tones, she added, 'Apart from the obvious, of course.'

Warwick seemed about to reply in kind, then his face became expressionless. Taking her case out of her hand, he said, 'We've been all though this particular conversation before.'

Lauren stood for a moment looking at him, wrenchingly aware that if this was to be her last time with him she wanted it to be untarnished. He had paused to look back at her, his brows lifting as she made no move to follow. Her heart seemed to lurch and she said simply, 'I'm sorry. Forget I said that.'

His expression softened, then his free hand pulled her

towards him and he kissed the top of her head. She had time to wonder briefly if he had ever made a similar gesture towards Petra or Vivian before he pushed her ahead of him through the door.

In the car they spoke little until they had left London behind them. Warwick swore mildly at the traffic congestion, but he seemed resigned, resting his arm idly on the door at the endless traffic lights.

When they were clear of the city and picking up speed, he lit a cigarette without taking his eyes from the road, and said, 'I think you'll like Rachel. And as James will be at his conciliatory best, you might even like him as well.'

'That sounds ominous,' Lauren observed.

He sent her a sideways glance, his mouth curved. 'Sitting in on a couple of board meetings with him might make you appreciate my tractable disposition, but as this is a purely social occasion as far as you're concerned he shouldn't trouble you.'

'Not entirely social. There are certain duties I was engaged for. How . . .' She hesitated, then rushed on, 'How close are we supposed to be?'

'Very.'

She stiffened, and his tone dry, Warwick said, 'I don't think Tessa would be deterred by anything else.'

She digested this in silence for a moment, and he said, 'I'd better fill you in on a few details before we get there. The house is actually my parents' old home where we were all brought up. When Rachel got married she was the last of us to leave, and my mother wanted somewhere smaller, so Rachel and James took it over. They have two sons, Howard nine and Michael seven, and a daughter, Karen, five.'

'Surname?' Lauren queried.

'Meynell.'

It struck a chord, but she couldn't quite pin it down, and Warwick said casually, 'James, no doubt to encourage his export efforts, was made a Knight of the most excellent Order of the British Empire, but we shall all be on completely informal terms, so you don't even need to think about it.'

Aware of increasing nervousness, Lauren said tartly, 'Thank you for mentioning it anyway. Is there anything else I should know?'

'I presume Tessa will be using her married name, which is Cunningham, but her father is Charles Tennant.'

'Tennant Enterprises?' She could feel the spread of fright as he nodded. Fenmore's was a powerful company, but the Tennant empire was international. Appalled, she burst out, 'You deliberately didn't tell me any of this before!'

She saw his mouth twitch and knew the charge was true, but he only shrugged and said, 'It doesn't make any difference.'

For a while she was speechless, brain and tongue paralysed, and feeling her temples grow damp at the prospect of the evening ahead. In a choked voice, she said, 'I can't possibly carry this off. Tessa isn't going to believe for a moment that you're serious about someone like me!'

Coolly, Warwick asked, 'Why not?'

'Why?' Lauren repeated helplessly. 'Because ... because I don't look or sound the part. I . . .'

She tailed off and he looked across at her quickly. 'I think you do, which is all that matters. You're beautiful, you've got more brains than Tessa and you'll be dressed for the part.' He sent her another quick look. 'You didn't buy that cream dress on the salary I pay you, even though it is fairly good. I know something about the price of women's clothes, and it was expensive.'

'It was given to me by the woman I used to work for,' Lauren told him.

She saw his sharply questioning look fade and he reached under the dash and handed her a small package. 'Here, I nearly forgot. To complete your outfit.'

She unwrapped the box slowly, guessing it contained earrings, from the size. As she lifted the lid she gave a small exclamation. They were pearl droppers, set in exquisitely delicate gold filigree. The pearls had to be real—artificial ones would never be put in such a setting, and she felt her first pleasure die as she looked down at them. She couldn't even guess at the cost, but she knew she couldn't possibly accept them.

Divining her thoughts, Warwick said bluntly, 'They're the sort of things you'll be expected to wear, and you couldn't afford them yourself.'

Still lost for words, she took one of them out of the box and trailed it across her finger, and in matter-of-fact tones Warwick said, 'They're a very small outlay compared with what I expect to gain from this deal, so don't let it bother you.' He gave her a faint smile. 'Since it's in the course of business I might even find a way to make them tax-deductible.'

She didn't believe him, but she would have to appear to accept them for now, so she said huskily, 'In that case, thank you.' Occupied with her thoughts, she stared at them until the gold blurred under her blind gaze, and Warwick's voice recalled her.

'Put them away,' he told her. 'And you'd better take your watch off as well. Rachel will lend you one when we get there. She has them for every occasion.'

Her watch was plain and functional, obviously out of keeping with her role, so she slipped it from her wrist without argument and asked, 'Does your sister know who I am?'

'That you're my secretary? Yes.'

He didn't expand on his reply, and with a spurt of

irritation she said, 'You know that isn't really what I meant. Does she know the reason I'm going?'

'Yes,' he repeated. She caught an inflection in his voice and looked at him quickly, but his dark eyes were narrowed in a smile and he said, 'Put your shoes back on. We're nearly there.'

She obeyed, wondering if she ever did anything without him noticing. Having eased her feet back in she looked up to find they had turned into a drive, wooded along one side so that she couldn't see where it led. When they left the trees behind the house was revealed ahead of them. Lauren took in the impressive stone façade and felt her stomach move with trepidation.

Making her tone light, she said, 'I hope you're not going to regret this. I feel I ought to tell you I've never stayed in a house with columns before.'

'Don't let it worry you. It's probably steeped in history, but none of it's ours. My father bought it when I was about four, complete with cockroaches.' Warwick braked smoothly to a halt in front of the shallow steps, adding, 'Thank God for modern pesticides!'

Slightly reassured by his irreverent attitude, Lauren gave him a wavering smile, and he said, 'You concentrate on your dress and I'll bring the cases.'

As they mounted the steps, Lauren wondered if there would be a butler—it seemed the sort of place which ought to have one, but the front door was slightly ajar and Warwick pushed it open with his foot without bothering to ring the ornate bell-pull. Inside, he dumped their cases and said, 'I'll find Rachel. If she appears before I do, introduce yourself. She's five feet eight and looks vaguely like me.'

He disappeared through an arched doorway at the rear of the carpeted and furnished hall, and Lauren stood nervously holding the plastic-covered dress. She hoped no one would come out and find her, and was relieved when Warwick returned with Rachel. The resemblance was so marked that it was unmistakable and gave Lauren the eerie feeling of knowing her already.

She smiled hesitantly, and Rachel said, 'Only my brother would leave you standing in the hall! Come on through and we'll have some tea or coffee or whatever. You're arrived at the best time, actually. The others are still out.'

Talking, she led the way into a room at the front of the house and collapsed into a chintz-covered armchair, gesturing to Lauren to take the settee. She had all Warwick's good looks and some of his manner, but in her the arrogance was tempered to a casual assurance that was more attractive.

'How's it going?' Warwick enquired. He crossed to the sideboard and took the stopper out of a decanter, sniffing the contents before pouring some into a glass. His amused gaze took in Rachel's abandoned pose as she stared up at the ceiling in mock exhaustion, and he held up the decanter. 'Shall I pour you one?'

'Please. What about Lauren?'

He grinned. 'She's not having any. And for God's sake warn James not to keep re-filling her glass at dinner, or you'll see why!'

'Does he usually slander you?' asked Rachel, her finely arched black brows lifting.

'He isn't,' Lauren told her. 'He knows I've absolutely no head for it.'

As she said it she felt heat run up her face. For a moment Rachel regarded her curiously, then she turned back to Warwick and remarked with affectionate malice, 'Your sins might catch up with you tonight, brother.'

Glass in hand, Warwick leaned back against the sideboard. 'For your information, my dear Rachel, I have never sinned in that particular quarter. I don't tangle with marrieds.'

Unkindly, she said, 'Then you must have made quite an impression on her. I think she's looking on this dinner as an opportunity for single-minded pursuit.'

Warwick took a swallow from his drink. 'Didn't you tell her I was bringing Lauren?'

'Oh, I told her.' Rachel stretched her legs out negligently in front of her and studied her gold-painted toenails. 'But I don't think she took it very seriously.'

'Then let's hope she restrains herself in front of her father.'

'I warn you that's a vain hope, Rick.' He looked across at her sharply and she spread her hands. 'He's been holding off all week, waiting for you to get here before he would enter into any real discussion. He seems to favour a private merger as well.' She shrugged. 'He keeps his age a secret, but he's bound to be over sixty and Tessa's his only child. You're a bright light at the moment, and I think he feels he'd like to retire and leave it all in a son-in-law's hands.'

'Then he can think again,' Warwick said curtly. He turned away and lit a cigarette, while Rachel watched him speculatively.

'It's not such a bad idea,' she pointed out. 'You gain in a day what it will take you ten years to achieve on your own, and Tessa's a reasonable bargain—the perfect hostess, and she's been using the children to demonstrate what an ideal mother she'll make.' She paused. 'Presumably you intend to get married one day. If you haven't succumbed for the usual reasons by the age of thirty-seven, you might as well take Tessa.'

'I'll do my own choosing and make my own way!'

His tone was brusque, and Rachel said lightly, 'No need to scowl at me—I was only suggesting it, not promoting it. All I ask is that you extricate yourself as diplomatically as possible. If the deal falls through I'd rather James wasn't able to say it was my brother's fault. The mantle of his displeasure falls heavily on occasions, and I have to live with him.'

Warwick's glance slid to Lauren. She had been listening to the conversation numbly, a silent outsider, and taking in her carefully blank expression, Warwick said deliberately, '—— James! If it falls through it falls through!'

Rachel raised mocking eyes. 'Tut, Rick! You're speaking of the man I love and probably shocking Lauren as well.'

'She's heard me before. She works for me, don't forget.'

'Yes,' said Lauren. 'But you usually close your door before expressing yourself quite so freely.'

He grinned at her. For a moment she was held by the warm amusement in his gaze, then she glanced at Rachel and caught her intrigued regard. There was a second of silent awareness and Lauren felt herself flush, then they heard the sounds of car doors slamming, and Rachel said, 'Damn, they're back. Rick, take Lauren up to her room and I'll have some tea sent up to her. She'll never get a chance to relax if they corner her now.'

Lauren wondered how she was to avoid being trapped since the other guests were already in the hall, but Warwick led her through a door into an adjoining room which came out by the servant's staircase at the rear of the house. Halfway along the upper landing he opened a door and signed her to go in. Still clutching her dress, she obeyed, and laid it on the bed before going over to the window.

In the foreground the gardens were immaculately kept, but the far end of the lawn was used as a cricket pitch and she could see three small figures vainly trying to rescue a ball from a large black labrador. It dashed into the bushes, and Lauren smiled at the distant shouts of frustration before turning back to Warwick.

He grinned at the scene. 'They've been trying to teach him to field, but he hasn't quite got the idea yet. I can see I shall have to give them some further assistance.' With a final glance through the window he stepped back and pushed open a white-panelled door. 'Your bathroom is here. We've got just over an hour until dinner. I'll come and get you on the way down.'

Immediately Lauren's anxiety returned and he moved towards her and pressed his knuckles lightly under her chin. 'Don't worry! You can cope.'

She smiled uncertainly. 'You have more faith than I do.'

'I need to have.'

His enigmatic gaze met her troubled one for a moment, then he brought his lips down on hers. She quivered against him, her reaction instant to the probing pressure, and his hands spread on her hips, thumbs digging into the bones as he pulled her to him. He raised his head after a while and traced his finger round her mouth before sliding his hand down to her throat and onward to cup her breast. She snatched a sharp breath at the lingering touch, her lids drooping, and Warwick muttered, 'I'd like to say to hell with all this and take you back home with me.'

She managed a strained smile. 'Rachel would kill you.'

'And you wouldn't come anyway.'

Lauren shook her head, biting her lip as his hand still moved on her, finger and thumb delicately plucking through the thin silk of her shirt.

'But you'd like to,' he said, watching the play of emotions reflected in her face. 'Otherwise you'd stop me from doing this now.'

'It's hardly the same thing.' She tried to pull away,

but his hand clamped into the small of her back. 'Let me go, Warwick. You've surely got enough candidates for what you want.'

'Yes,' he agreed. 'So doesn't that tell you something?'

'Perhaps that you're not used to meeting with resistance and you don't like being beaten.'

'That's not a valid conclusion and you know it. There have been two occasions when you didn't offer any resistance. I could have taken you then if I'd only been concerned with what I wanted myself.'

It was true, and with the pressure of his hand forcing her against him she could feel that same desire licking through her again. Fighting the weakness, she pushed against his chest with her fists and repeated, 'Let me go! Rachel said she was having some tea sent up.'

Warwick held her a moment longer, then relaxed his grip and she stepped back. Watching her with a faint smile, he said, 'Perhaps you're right—the place but not the time. I'll call back for you in an hour.'

When he had gone Lauren allowed her control to slip and lay for a while on the bed imagining what it would be like to go back with him to his apartment and let him make love to her. Longing surged through her, unchecked, until she reminded herself of the difference in what it would mean to them. To Warwick it would be physical release, while she would be surrendering her very soul.

The thought brought back some measure of calm and she got up and unpacked the few things in her bag. Her tea arrived as she finished, and when she had drunk it she showered and dressed with deliberate slowness, keeping her movements unhurried in an attempt to quieten her nerves.

When Warwick knocked she felt as though she was as ready as she ever would be. He came in, closing the door against the sound of voices on the landing, and picked up her left hand to fasten a small gold watch on her wrist. It was set round with tiny diamonds, and assailed by fresh nerves she tested the clasp.

'It's got a strong safety chain, and anyway it's insured,' Warwick told her.

Lauren nodded dumbly, in no way reassured, and he stood looking at her for a moment, then led her across the room and faced her towards the mirror, holding her from behind with his hands lightly on her upper arms.

'Take a good look,' he said. 'That's what everyone sees, so remember it.'

She did as he ordered, marvelling that her face could appear so composed. It was as though she was studying someone else, a poised stranger, with remote, amber-flecked eyes and a curtain of dark red hair. She swallowed, and suddenly the stranger was herself again and she saw that her face was so pale it showed up the faint scattering of normally invisible freckles.

She met Warwick's eyes in the mirror. Even in her very high heels he was still a head taller, and he seemed bigger and darker than ever in the black dinner jacket.

She gave him a trembling smile. 'I feel totally unprepared for this. Do I say I'm your secretary?'

'Make it personal assistant.' His answering smile held cynicism. 'A rose by any other name, but perhaps it sounds more impressive. Just follow my lead. I'll stick with you as much as I can.'

His hands tightened momentarily in encouragement, and resigned, she picked up her evening bag. 'Lead me to the slaughter, then.'

They went down the wide, branching staircase, and in the hall Warwick guided her, a hand on her back, towards an open doorway from which she could hear voices and laughter.

Inside, she paused. She supposed it was what would be termed a drawing room in a house of this age and size. The colours in the mainly pink and blue Aubusson carpet were reflected in the ornate, gilded plasterwork of the ceiling, and four tall French doors stood open on to the gardens at the rear of the house. Lauren gained only a swift impression of the group round the flower-filled marble fireplace before Rachel detached herself and came to meet them.

She gave Lauren a narrowed, conspiratorial smile and said, 'Good luck,' before turning to Warwick. 'Introduce her round and get her a drink, Rick.'

He nodded, and Lauren's eyes were drawn to the group by the fireplace again. She tried to sort out which of the three women would be Tessa, but Warwick said, 'It might be polite to let our host meet you first.' He raised his voice slightly. 'James?'

His brother-in-law turned, excusing himself from the conversation, and Lauren tensed as he approached them. By no means a handsome man, he was nearer fifty than forty, and though he lacked Warwick's impressive height he was equally broad. He emanated power, both mental and physical, and Lauren knew Warwick had been waiting for her instinctive recoil when his fingers pressed into her back, propelling her forward.

She saw the other man's eyes flick, taking in the almost invisible movement. Sir James Meynell, she thought, would miss very little, but he welcomed her smoothly, his handshake firm, manners polished.

He had a surprisingly beautiful voice, at odds with his formidable appearance, and listening to his brief exchange with Warwick, Lauren began to realise how far she was out of her depth. The mere possession of wealth had never awed her—a lot of the men Warwick dealt with were very wealthy indeed and they didn't particularly impress her, but she was suddenly aware of her own background by comparison. The social graces she had so painstakingly learned, these people acquired unconsciously from the cradle, and though her speech was without accent, the faint traces of her Bradford origins having long since faded, here she still stood out. Among his own kind, the suggestion of public school in Warwick's tones was emphasised, and it was brought forcibly home to her that they were more widely divided than by just the gulf between a rich business man and his secretary.

The courage lent by her expensive dress and earrings deserted her, and when their host left them to attend to the drinks, she asked quietly, 'Warwick, what does your father do?'

He glanced down at her quickly, his gaze considering, then shrugged. 'Grows roses and collects antique firearms.'

'I shall be expected to know. I could be made to look a fool here tonight if I don't.'

She knew he sensed what had prompted the question, and he hesitated, then said, 'All right. As we tell him frequently, in spite of the general reaction it's nothing to be ashamed of. He's a judge. Rachel and the rest of us tended not to advertise it unnecessarily when we were younger—in some company it can put a complete blight on the conversation.'

Lauren could well imagine it. Warwick knew perfectly well that if she had known everything that was entailed, nothing on earth would have persuaded her to come.

Taking a deep breath, she said, 'Is there anything else I should know in case I make a total idiot of myself?'

'I don't think so,' he replied evenly. 'Is there anything you should tell me, for the same reason?'

Her eyes flew to his face, then fell away again. A flush staining her cheeks she said stiffly, 'I wouldn't have thought there was any danger of that.'

'Wouldn't you?' he returned, his voice dry. 'Perhaps you haven't realised how we're playing this scene.'

He moved forward as he spoke, and concealing quivering nerves, Lauren smiled at the enquiring faces turned towards them. It was one of those odd breaks which sometimes occur in conversation, all talk ceasing at the same time. Even in normal circumstances it was unnerving enough to be the object of so many curious eyes. She felt now that she must have 'impostor' written all over her. Her mind blanked, she continued to smile mechanically as she was introduced to two beautifully dressed women before they came at last to Charles Tennant and Tessa.

For a moment her attention was held by Charles, the strength of his personality dominating. Like all the men in the room he gave an impression of power, and behind his friendly expression his eyes were chill and calculating. It frightened Lauren to realise that he would believe she was responsible for thwarting the plans he held for Warwick and his daughter. In spite of Rachel's revelations when they arrived, Lauren hadn't really grasped that there was anyone but Tessa involved. Now she turned to her almost with relief as the less disturbing figure.

Perhaps thirty, she was an elegant, natural blonde. Not beautiful by the standard of perfect features, she reminded Lauren of Renaissance paintings of the Madonna, except that the serenity was missing from her expression. Her answering smile was forced, and filling an awkward gap, Warwick said easily, 'I haven't seen you since God knows when. One of the spring race meetings, wasn't it?'

'Yes. Daddy had his new filly running.'

It had obviously cost her an effort to match his light tones, and dragging her gaze away from his face she met Lauren's eyes again, hostility showing briefly before she managed to banish it.

Lauren was uncomfortably aware of Warwick's hand still resting on her waist. Until meeting Tessa she had had a hazy impression of someone spoiled and predatory—a privileged woman reaching out for something she wanted and prepared to use any means.

The reality was an unpleasant shock. Privileged she undoubtedly was, and perhaps spoiled as well, Lauren had no means of knowing, but her motive for persuading her father to exert this discreet blackmail was painfully clear. She was almost sick with love for Warwick. As they chatted, Warwick enquiring after the progress of Charles's racehorses, her eyes returned continually to his face, betraying a hunger all her upbringing and pride could not conceal.

Lauren could appreciate Warwick's difficulty now. Had he come alone tonight, Tessa's desperation would have made her both embarrassing and pathetic. Warwick would have been forced into the position of either humiliating her by politely rebuffing her, or sparing her in public and creating even greater difficulties for himself later when the deal was discussed. To parade another woman in front of her seemed cruel, but it was the most tactful measure.

Feeling sorry for her made Lauren's role harder. She realised she had nothing to fear in the way of jealous scenes—manners would always prevail in this well-bred gathering, but equally, any overt display of affection between herself and Warwick would be frowned on. She left it to Warwick to convey the message, which he did unmistakably by his air of total ownership. He seldom left her side, his hand under her arm proprietorial as he steered her round the room, talking easily on everything, and adroitly diverting any questions which threatened to become awkward.

Gradually Lauren began to relax, helped probably by the sherry, she realised when she discovered her glass was empty. She saw Warwick give it an idle glance, and when there was no one within earshot he bent over her and murmured, 'I'm going to fetch you another one, but it's for decorative purposes only!'

She laughed up at him and met the warmth in his expression. His fingers slid down her arm and tightened briefly on her hand in a gesture of reassurance before he crossed the room to where the drinks and glasses were laid out on a marble topped cabinet.

Returning, he handed her the sherry and said, 'One sip for appearances' sake, and remember that it's your Achilles heel and go easy on the wine at dinner.' He looked down at her for a moment, a half smile playing on his lips. 'Though in different circumstances the effects are highly desirable!'

It was a deliberate reminder of the night she had spent in his bed, and she felt a sudden clutch in the pit of her stomach and a spreading heat which rose up her body and finally coloured her face. She knew she was proclaiming her feelings as clearly as Tessa, and when she looked up his dark eyes were brilliant with lingering amusement, and a stronger, more basic emotion that constricted her breath.

He said softly, 'Yes, memory can be a powerful aphrodisiac, can't it?'

Staring at her glass to hide her confusion, she heard him laugh, and in the same soft tones he said, 'At this moment I'd like to take you upstairs and kiss you senseless.' He paused and she felt him studying her. 'Tessa is watching and you're giving a very convincing performance. While she's looking, shall I tell you what else I'd like to do to you?'

He was weaving a spell round her, his words intentionally evocative, and Lauren felt a surge of resentment because he could rouse her to such a pitch without even touching her. Sharply, she said, 'I don't think it's very—kind to mock her.'

'Oh, I'm not mocking her, believe me. If Rachel and I appear to it's because we're uncomfortable. I'm sorry for her, but what the hell can I do about it?' His tone hardening, he said, 'I sympathise even more because she's going through what I have myself these last months, watching you and knowing damned well what reaction I'd get if I overstepped your invisible line. At least I've never slapped her down the way you did me when I made my one and only overture!'

She flushed and returned defensively, 'It was hardly the same thing.'

'How do you know?' he asked, his tone sardonic. 'You've no God-given insight that tells you how I feel, and outright rejection wounds the pride if nothing else.'

Something in the way he spoke sent tremors of alarm through her. Hesitantly, she said, 'I didn't think there was anything more than pride involved.'

'Didn't you?' he asked. 'How about an exchange of confidences? You tell me what it is that you're so determined to keep hidden, and in return I'll tell you exactly what *is* involved.'

He watched her shy violently away from the suggestion and demanded, 'Which is it? You don't want to know or you don't want to tell me?'

After a pause she said, 'Both.'

Warwick nodded as though it was the reply he had expected. 'How long are we going to go on fencing?'

'Please, Warwick!' she muttered desperately. 'It isn't something we can talk about here!'

His glance ranged round the room and returned to her troubled face. 'Agreed. Smile—you're looking too serious.'

She obeyed, and with an abrupt change of mood he leaned over and said, 'And I'd still like to take you upstairs and kiss you senseless.' When she looked up at him his eyes were half veiled by the thick lashes, and laughing silently, he added, 'And I don't need to tell you the rest.'

Lauren began to think dinner would never come. Warwick's outward manner was perfectly correct, but the echo of his softly uttered statement fanned the physical awareness between them until she felt it was so obvious it could be plucked out of the air. Tessa's dull regard disturbed her, and her embarrassment increased when she discovered James's speculative gaze fixed on her as well. She flushed. He and Rachel both knew why she was here, but they must have realised this was more than just an act put on for Tessa's benefit. James's considering eyes moved slowly to Warwick, a few yards away, then returned to Lauren. He was a man who would never allow his expression to reveal anything against his will, and Lauren was shaken to read the coolness there.

Bewildered, she wondered why. Did he think she was Warwick's mistress? He surely knew Warwick would never have brought her to stay if she was. His love life might overlap at work, but he would keep it strictly separate from his family.

It struck her then that James's disapproval might be because he believed the reverse—the classic situation of the secretary managing to hook the boss, but he must also know that was just as improbable. Or was it? With sudden doubt she remembered Warwick's earlier words which she had nervously pushed to the back of her mind. It was impossible, she told herself. It had to be impossible, or she was unable to contemplate the magnitude of her own guilt.

Somehow she survived the meal, barely tasting the salmon mousse and saddle of lamb. She still had a part to play and she smiled and talked, but the spontaneous spark was gone and she was consciously acting now. When they all returned to the drawing room Warwick tried to hold her back in the hall, but she pulled her arm free and walked in after the others.

The blue brocade curtains had been drawn while they were eating, and the room was lit by two chandeliers of Venetian glass, which for some reason made the women look pale. Lauren caught sight of herself in one of the gilded mirrors. Her freckles were showing again, and Warwick knew her too well to believe that the lighting was the only reason for her pallor.

He cornered her eventually, manoeuvring so that his back was to the rest of the room and shielding her, then demanded, 'What's the matter?'

Refusing to meet his eyes, she said steadily, 'Nothing.'

'Nothing, or something else you can't tell me here?'

She wondered if there was ever a right time for telling him she didn't aspire to what his brother-in-law suspected—and disapproved of. She should have listened to Ann and told him about Mandy before. But even if it hadn't been for Mandy she knew she didn't fit in here. She'd spent most of the evening listening because she couldn't join in with talk of sailing, and the imminent cubbing season, and bringing hunters up from grass. Warwick had rescued her when she was asked if she played golf.

But she couldn't say baldly, 'If you were thinking of marrying me, there's a reason why you can't.' He hadn't asked her, and it could be something entirely different he had in mind. Bringing her here might have been to serve a double purpose. The one motive was genuine enough—he would certainly have been in trouble with Tessa, but he could also have been demonstrating that she could never have any official part in his life. He wanted her, and she no longer believed he was only interested in one of his usual affairs, but she wasn't wife material either.

She met his eyes with a strained half smile, and said truthfully, 'I've got rather a headache. This is beginning to get me down.'

Warwick examined her face frowningly. 'I'll find you something for it.' The frown faded, warmth returning. 'Stick it out. It won't go on for much longer.'

The headache was real enough. For a while Lauren was afraid it would develop into a full-scale migraine, but the aspirin Warwick brought her eased it, and Rachel drifted up, murmuring, 'Don't worry. I'll have them all cleared out in half an hour, then you can go to bed. The men don't want us around anyway when they get down to business.'

'True,' Warwick agreed, grinning at her.

'We leave them to get on with it in a dense atmosphere of cigar smoke and Paco Rabanne,' said Rachel with a grimace.

The smell of wealth, Lauren thought wryly, getting ready for bed. And far removed from the odours of damp and cooking which characterised the building where she lived.

What *did* Warwick want from her? She lay back against the pillows, sifting and weighing separate incidents, some small, some significant. But they could all be read different ways, just as her presence here could. Perhaps Warwick hoped to make her his mistress in the style of the old courtesans, accepted and semi-respectable—a secure position and a pension when there were no longer any duties to fulfil. She had almost convinced herself when she remembered James's expression. It brought her up with a jolt, flooding her with guilt.

Slow, warm tears slid from beneath her closed eyelids as she faced what she had known all along. She had to get away—right away, not just from Fenmore's. The situation was impossible from every angle and it would be better to make a completely fresh start somewhere else. She wouldn't be Warwick's mistress and she couldn't be his wife, so all her agonising was pointless. It didn't matter which role he had in mind for her—both of them were out.

She heard quiet footsteps on the landing outside and looked at her watch. Ten minutes to two. The discussion downstairs must have broken up. Softly spoken goodnights confirmed it, and a light was switched off, leaving only a pale shaft to shine under her door.

She lay and stared at it, dry eyed now, but with lids that felt stiff. Her holidays were coming up, so she had two weeks in which to reorganise herself. She had faced worse things in the past. No, that wasn't true. More frightening perhaps—the terrifying moment when she had first acknowledged that she could be pregnant, when she had told her mother, when Trevor deserted her. They had all made her sick with fright, but none of them had left her with the feeling she had now in this voluntary tearing apart of herself.

There was a faint click and the shaft of light widened, showing Warwick silhouetted in the doorway. Lauren raised herself quickly on to her elbow, and seeing her movement he switched on the wall brackets and soundlessly closed the door behind him.

For a long moment she stared at him, feeling her whole body thud to the beat of her heart, then she shook her head, whispering, 'No!'

He crossed the room and sat on the edge of the bed, his bare feet silent on the carpet. Dark blue pyjamas showed beneath his robe, but the exposed area of his chest revealed that he wasn't wearing the jacket. Her eyes were held by the black hair thickening down to his stomach, and she swallowed, and in a low voice protested, 'You said . . . you told me Rachel . . .'

'It's three o'clock and the whole house is asleep.' His smile twisted. 'Except for you and me. I couldn't sleep for thinking of you only three doors away along the landing. What's your reason?'

Because of him, though her thoughts had been very different.

Desperately, she said, 'Go back, Warwick! Someone may hear us, and this is your sister's house!'

He shook his head. 'Your bathroom is on one side of us and there's a dressing room on the other. We shan't be heard.'

Lauren didn't need to ask why he had come, and the thought made her shake, churning her insides with a movement that left her weak. A treacherous voice in her brain whispered, 'Why not? Just this once for a memory you can take with you.' Trying to banish the temptation, she tightened every muscle in an effort to regain control.

'It doesn't make any difference. We're still in her house.'

'I don't care,' he told her flatly.

He reached out and slowly ran his fingers down the side of her face, his eyes searching for the response he wanted. Lauren lowered her lashes against him, afraid of what he could see, then felt herself pressed back on to the bed. Her struggles were stilled by the weight of his body, protest stifled by his lips. Resistance ebbed and died as his mouth moved on hers, coaxing it apart for his exploration, while his hands slid beneath her, impatiently pushing up her thin nightdress so he could feel the warmth of her bared flesh. Needles of fire went through her, building into a heated desire that made her twist against him, and with a stifled exclamation he raised himself and snatched her nightdress over her head, tugging it down over her arms to fling it on to the floor behind him.

Naked, and without the covering of the bedclothes, she felt a cool draught from the window that brought her temporarily to her senses. The sudden chill recalled her long enough for her to realise that this time Warwick had no intention of keeping himself in check. Always before there had been restraint, an exercise of control that held him short of the ultimate danger point, but now he was giving free rein to his desire. There was a tremor of urgency in his hands as they caressed her—open sensuality in the taut planes of his face.

The light, which should have been a friend, inhibiting her, proved her enemy. Her moment of doubt was revealed to him so that instantly his mouth was on hers again, his experienced fingers quickening the nerves in her breast, then smoothing down over her stomach to her thighs to send ripples of sensation coursing through her and smother the faint voice of sanity.

It was only when he paused to slide out of his clothes that fear returned. She stiffened and whispered, 'Warwick—no!' but he misunderstood the reason for her fear, murmuring persuasive reassurance and willing a response from her with his urgent touch.

Lauren was barely conscious of his words, the low, thickened tone of his voice touching a chord that brought a wild surge of panic. She tried to push him away, but he pinned her down, trapping her threshing legs with his own so that she was made aware of his enormous strength and her own complete helplessness. Struggling frantically, she was transported back in time, mindless with fear and disgust as in her blurred perception Warwick merged with that other figure that, heedless of her pleas and resistance, had overpowered her and forced her to submit.

For a moment they were one in her mind, then Warwick's voice recalled her. Shaking her to penetrate her panic, he bent to touch her throat with his lips as he said huskily, 'Darling, listen to me!—We'll get married! As soon as you like we'll get married!'

She stared back at him, hectically flushed and panting, but so cold inside that she could clearly note the line of colour running across his cheekbones and the expanded pupils that proclaimed the depth of his desire. With the same clarity her brain registered that he had called her darling when he had never used any endearment to her before. That he had used, in fact, almost the identical words Trevor had, when in the grip of the same overriding lust he had been prepared to promise her anything that might gain him her willing body.

Shaking with sickness, her voice vibrant with contempt and loathing, she cried out, '*No!*' and twisted violently away from him.

CHAPTER EIGHT

WARWICK froze, so still that after one sharp intake, even his breathing ceased. Then he rolled himself away from her and sat up, elbows resting on his knees. Lauren was still fighting to control the remnants of the stifling fear, snatching in lungfuls of air to overcome the sense of suffocation. The pulses in her temple beat heavily in unison with her throat, and the cool air from the window chilled the film of sweat that had formed in her hair and behind her ears. She ran the back of her hand under her bottom lip and saw it had come away wet, then looked up to meet Warwick's shuttered gaze.

In a voice devoid of expression, he said, 'So much for my first offer of marriage.'

As fear retreated the sense of his words gradually reached her and she realised what she had done. It was Trevor she had answered, not Warwick.

Clenching her hands, she struggled to a sitting position and dropped her head forward on to her arms. Warwick's voice seemed to come from a long way distant as he asked, 'Nothing to say? No trite comment appropriate to this situation?' With a savagery that jolted her to complete awareness, he added, 'But there's no need, is there? You've said it all!'

He let himself down on to one elbow so that he was facing her and she quickly looked away from the grim lines etched down between nose and mouth. In shaken tones she said at last, 'What do you want me to say?'

'Oh, nothing, my dear, nothing! You encompassed everything with a single word!' He paused, then went on viciously, 'I'd no idea until now that one commonplace syllable, two ordinary little letters, could possibly convey so much!'

With weary resignation she said, 'What did you expect?'

'For God's sake!' he exclaimed harshly. 'What sort of a question is that? What does any man expect, except that if it's a refusal it will at least be reasonably tactfully phrased!'

Using all her inner strength, she made her voice distant and said, 'Answer me one question and swear it will be the truth.'

She waited for his reply and he hesitated, then said briefly, 'All right.'

The words already framed in her mind, Lauren forced herself to utter them. 'When you came through that door tonight, was it with the intention of asking me to marry you?'

She had thought out the question, using words with care so that there could only be one reply if he answered her truthfully as he had promised.

The silence stretched. She heard him take a long breath, and finally he said, 'No.'

She plucked mindlessly at the lace on the edge of the pillow, not daring to look at him. 'Then there's nothing else for either of us to say.'

Abruptly Warwick got up and dressed again, reaching for her nightdress and tossing it on to the bed beside her. Lauren slipped it over her head, relieved to be covered from his bleak gaze. Her misery total, she knew she had achieved what she had earlier planned to do by flight. Nothing would ever erase from Warwick's mind the memory of that bitter, violent rejection. The one word had rung with a stark revulsion, utterly convincing because he knew it had been blind, unconscious reaction. No man's pride could take that. It was the ultimate insult.

'But it wasn't for you, Warwick,' she told him silently. 'It wasn't meant for you.'

It was an echo from another time, a revival of fear and disgust from another man's usage. But she couldn't tell him that. She had lived a lie with him too long. Disregarding her own warning instincts and Ann's advice, she had gone on concealing the insurmountable barrier between them. It might ease Warwick's pride if she told him the truth, but it wouldn't achieve anything else. At least this way he would never be tortured as she was by things that might have been.

His curt tones breaking into her thoughts, he said, 'I don't think either of us is capable of maintaining this fiction over breakfast, so I suggest we leave before the others are up. I have to come back, so I'll make your excuses and give some explanation.'

'Very well,' she agreed drearily.

He left without another word. Lauren wondered if he intended to wake her and knew it wouldn't be necessary. There was no possibility of sleep and already the sky was beginning to grow lighter. When he tapped on the door she was dressed, her case packed, and he showed no surprise to find she was ready. They drank orange juice and coffee in the kitchen, then they left.

In the car he said, 'Fasten your safety-belt,' but they were the only words he spoke during the entire journey. Lauren kept her eyes closed most of the way, opening them when the stopping and starting told her they had reached the city's snarled traffic. Warwick drove grimly, thrusting the car into gear and accelerating away from lights in a way which made her catch her breath. He knew she was a nervous passenger, and it was only by rigid control that she prevented exclamations of alarm as he drove with the front bumper nearly touching the car in front. She wondered if he was doing it deliberately or he was merely uncaring.

When they neared the flat, the tears she had been holding back threatened to overcome her. She could feel his bitter thoughts filling the car, as tangible as words, and unable to bear it any longer, she broke out, 'Warwick, I . . .' She faltered to a halt, then finished pleadingly, 'It wasn't as it sounded.'

His features were a carved mask, only his eyes betraying scorn as he turned to look at her.

'Don't bother,' he told her, barely suppressed anger threaded in his tone. 'You've already offered me one sop to injured pride, but you said everything else. With admirable conciseness!' he added savagely.

Lowering her lashes to hide the hurt and the tears, Lauren slipped the box containing the pearl earrings on to the parcel shelf and got out without a backward glance. The passenger door was barely closed before Warwick drove away, loose gravel scattering the path from his violent acceleration.

It was still barely nine o'clock and Ann wasn't up. Putting her case down quietly in the bedroom, Lauren saw her stir and said, 'Would you like a cup of tea?'

Receiving a muffled assent, she went to the kitchen to make it, moving like an automaton, numb from lack of sleep and the emotional wound. She carried the tray back in, and Ann said cheerfully, 'And how was your evening with the upper ten thousand?'

With her back turned, Lauren said, 'Fine,' and it wasn't until she took the cup over that Ann saw her stricken expression. With a tremor in her voice, Lauren said, 'Don't ask me any more—not yet.'

'Oh,' Ann said flatly. 'I . . . no, all right. Say the word when you're ready.'

Lauren nodded, and blank with fatigue, took her skirt off and lay on the bed. After a while, Ann tactfully got up and left her, and she lay staring at the ceiling and wondering why she could no longer cry now that she wanted to.

Images of Warwick revolved round in her mind—she hadn't realised until now how minutely she knew his features and his every expression. Each plane and angle of his face was familiar to her, the heavy-lidded dark eyes, slightly Roman nose, the suggestion of a wave in the black hair that she had vaguely noticed needed cutting. She tried to push the pictures away, but they returned, and she thought suddenly that she knew why people committed suicide. It wasn't death they were seeking, but oblivion—a respite from something that had become unendurable.

She got up again eventually and pulled on a pair of jeans, afterwards fastening her hair back with the wooden clasp that Warwick so despised. In the mirror her face was pale, but she had regained her composure when she went to look for Ann.

She was sitting outside in one of the aged deckchairs, her skirt pulled up to expose her legs to the sun. Lauren dropped down beside her on the grass, and said after a moment, 'Ann, what would you do if I left?'

'It's as bad as that, is it?'

She looked down and saw Lauren's affirming nod, searching her face before she said slowly, 'Divorce Tony and marry Mac, probably.'

'Haven't you before because of me?'

Ann hesitated. 'Not exactly. It's more that I needed a push to make up my mind. I know Tony's never coming back, but I've gone on waiting a bit longer and then a bit longer, and Mac might possibly lose patience with me one day.' Her gaze fixed on the backs of the houses beyond the end of the garden, identical to their own, even to the grime. 'To tell you the truth, I'm getting sick of this view and I'm not sure I can face another

winter in our bedroom. Mac can afford to put down a
reasonable deposit on a house, and frankly I shouldn't
wait for a wedding ring to move in.' She looked down
at Lauren again. 'So you've decided to cut and run. Is
that absolutely final?'

'Yes,' said Lauren with resolution.

Without the information she had just gained, she
suspected that she might have weakened, compromised
in some way, but it would have been fatal. She could
imagine herself lurking in doorways outside Fenmore's
just to catch a glimpse of Warwick. She remembered
the curious feeling she'd had when she read Mrs
Munro's letter that she was being impelled towards
change. A portent of doom.

During the weekend she made a determined effort to
fight through her depression, deliberately occupying
every waking moment. It was easier when Mandy came
back. For her sake, she had to maintain an outward
cheerfulness, and she found it was a good discipline.

She'd had long discussions with Ann and they agreed
they wouldn't say anything to the two children until
some definite arrangements had been made, but they
would start weaning them from each other's company.
They had been like sisters for the last two years,
automatically assuming that any treat or outing for one
of them included the other. They were bound to be
upset when they learned they were to be separated,
though Sarah would have the consolation of belonging
in a normal family background at last.

Lauren still had no idea what her own future would
be. She reflected that their caravan holiday couldn't
have come at a worse time. It would cost money she
could ill afford now, and there would be an entire week
when she couldn't seriously plan anything.

But Mandy was looking forward to it with bubbling
enthusiasm, so Lauren took her shopping for beach

clothes and tried to work up some interest in her own holiday wear. In the end she just bought a cotton skirt and a couple of sun-tops. She didn't bother with a costume because she couldn't swim.

Hot and laden with their purchases, they caught the bus home, getting off by the dusty little park at the end of their road. Mandy wanted an icecream, so Lauren waited patiently while she queued at the kiosk. The park was crowded because of the school holidays and hot weather, and if anything there seemed to be more fathers than mothers accompanying the children. She saw Mandy watching one man pushing his two little girls on the swings, and wondered how much sense of loss her daughter felt.

When Mandy rejoined her with her chosen icecream, she wasn't surprised when she suddenly demanded, 'Is my daddy nice?'

'No,' Lauren thought bitterly. 'He's a swine without the guts to take the responsibility for what he did. He's never even seen you because he left before you were born, and I thank God daily that you don't bear the remotest resemblance to him.'

She looked down to see Mandy watching her expectantly, and forced a smile. What could you say to a child of six? Almost choked by the words, she replied lightly, 'Of course he's nice, darling.'

'If he was here, would he push me on the swings like that man did?'

'I expect so,' said Lauren. She could see from Mandy's expression that there were more questions coming. She braced herself to parry them, but at that moment a large piece of the melting icecream fell off the side of the cornet, and Mandy let out an outraged wail.

Lauren quickly dissuaded her from trying to rescue it from the pavement, and for a few seconds Mandy glared at the spreading pool, then ran on ahead to hide behind the letter box. Relieved that her questions were forgotten, Lauren smiled. She knew Mandy would be holding her breath, waiting to jump out on her and shout, 'Boo!' She was completely unaware of the fact that her short yellow skirt was sticking out behind the pillar box.

Lauren obligingly started and feigned fright when she was supposed to, and Mandy went ahead to repeat the game, crouching down behind their next door neighbour's wall with its convenient privet hedge.

Lauren was perhaps twenty yards away when she heard the unmistakable engine note of Warwick's Porsche. She walked on slowly with a curious sense of detachment for the inevitability of what must follow. As though in slow motion she saw the car stop and Warwick get out and go round to the front of the car to wait for her. Her eyes were fixed on him, her face completely blank, and he frowned quickly and took a step towards her. She heard Mandy's smothered giggle from behind the wall, and, her face still calm and smooth, she had time to reflect on how strange it was that the thing she had dreaded above all else now seemed completely unimportant.

Then Mandy jumped out, squealing with delight as she grabbed her round the waist. The sound was broken off as she saw Warwick standing by the car. Her arms tightened convulsively about Lauren, and half on a sob, she cried, 'Mummy!'

Lauren watched Warwick's eyes travel from herself to Mandy. For a moment they rested on her hair, then they returned again and his face slowly whitened with shock. She had never seen a man go pale before—even his lips were drained of all colour, and she wondered dispassionately if men ever felt faint in the same way women did.

She stood quite still, one hand on Mandy's shoulder,

reassuring and protective, then with startling suddenness he swung on his heel and strode back round the car. The door slammed and he was gone, and if it had not been for Mandy, frantically clutching her and sobbing, she could almost believe the brief scene had never taken place.

But Mandy was real enough and close to hysterics. Breaking out of her trance, Lauren picked her up and carried her inside to deposit her gently on her bed. Taking her hands, she knelt in front of her shushing and soothing. Mandy was far too distraught to answer questions. All she could say, over and over again, was, 'Don't let him come back, Mummy! Please don't let him come back!'

'He won't, darling,' Lauren assured her. Some other time she would find out why Mandy was so terrified of Warwick. He would never come back now.

After everything else that had happened, Lauren supposed she ought to have expected the holiday to be an unmitigated disaster as well.

The long spell of dry weather broke the day before, and they travelled down on the coach through a landscape obscured by driving rain. At the coach terminal they had difficulty getting a taxi, and when they arrived, drenched, at the caravan site, Lauren thought it was the dreariest place she had ever seen. Then when the rain eventually slackened off and they went to investigate the beach, Mandy was loud in her disappointment because it was pebbles.

'I'm a fool,' Lauren thought hopelessly. 'I should have asked. Children can't make sandcastles out of pebbles.'

There was a faintly unpleasant smell in the caravan and the state of the small Calor gas cooker made her wrinkle her nose in disgust. When she thought of spending a week in it she could have wept.

She unpacked their suitcases and stowed everything away. There was a sort of emergency ration kit left for them, bread, milk and essentials, but she didn't fancy preparing food until she'd cleaned the kitchen area, so she told Mandy they would go for a meal at the café she had noticed when they went out to look for the beach.

It wasn't bad, baked beans and chips with everything, but the prices were reasonable and she supposed their catering was geared to popular demand. Mandy ate the greasy chips with relish, making Lauren wonder why she bothered to drain them on kitchen paper at home.

She pushed her own meal round the plate until it was cold, trying to make her tired mind plan the week ahead. It was supposed to be a holiday—an enjoyable break for both of them, but her brain was too busy worrying about when the holiday was over. She had to find somewhere to live, a new job, transport their belongings, get Mandy into a new school—all the thousand and one things that moving entailed, and which at the moment she felt too drained to face.

Mandy was eating a bright red jelly with one eye on what she was doing and the other on a large family at the next table. The children were noisy and cheerful and not over-clean, and Mandy seemed fascinated by their uninhibited exchanges across the table. From time to time the smallest boy pulled a face at her, and indignantly Mandy pulled one back. Lauren hoped devoutly that they were not establishing a rapport.

Her fears were realised the next morning when there was a knock on the door while they were having breakfast. She opened it to the small, gap-toothed boy, and he said, 'Can she come to play?'

Her eyes bright, Mandy was away from the table like a shot, and Lauren looked at the small boy uncertainly.

'Well—I don't know. Where were you going to play?'

'Up the park,' he informed her. 'Me sister's coming as well. Me mum makes her.'

'How old is your sister?'

'Ten,' he supplied, adding, at the doubt in her face, 'coming up eleven.'

Resigned, Lauren said, 'All right. I'll come with you and see where it is.'

She put on her anorak and accompanied them to the play area beyond the café. There was an attendant in charge of it and it seemed fairly well supervised, so Lauren obtained a promise from Mandy that she would not leave the play park and said she would come back for her in an hour. Meeting the derisive gaze of Ben and his plump sister, she fixed them with a steely look and said, 'You're not to take her anywhere else, do you hear me?'

Ben said, 'Cross me 'eart and spit,' and Lauren shuddered inwardly when he suited the action to the words.

She left them and went to stock up at the small supermarket. The day was cold, with a grey, leaden sky, and the beach was completely deserted, the dark, oily waves making a depressing sound as they encroached, then hissed back from the pebbles. So much for her visions of sunshine and sandcastles, Lauren thought wryly.

She looked round with distaste at the empty crisp packets and chip papers blowing everywhere. The wire litter baskets were full to overflowing, and wasps buzzed round the apple cores and lolly sticks. Perhaps when the sun came out it would seem better, she told herself hopefully.

But the sun remained hidden and it got worse. On the third day of drizzling rain, Ben's parents came to ask if Mandy could go out with them, apologising because they hadn't got room in their battered car for her as well.

In the face of Mandy's eagerness Lauren didn't know how to refuse, and afterwards Mandy accompanied them everywhere automatically. They seemed to patronise nothing but amusement arcades and fairgrounds, and Mandy was constantly demanding more money. Lauren gave it to her, wincing at the thought of her hard-earned cash disappearing into slot machines.

Feeling a reluctant obligation, she had all four children to lunch on the last day. They cleared the food like a swarm of locusts, then looked round for more, and she went to the supermarket and bought a block of icecream and some sticky cakes. They demolished them noisily, then all disappeared without a word of thanks, leaving Lauren amid the chaos of dirty dishes and scattered crumbs.

Resentfully she cleared up after them, knowing Mandy was every bit as bad. She had given up correcting her speech and table manners. She would get her back to normal when she got home. At least she hoped she would. Mandy's only conversation seemed to be what Auntie Lil and Uncle Walter said and did, and their lightest utterances were treated as gospel.

As she finished washing up she noticed that for the first time the clouds were breaking up and the sky showed patches of blue. It would, she thought bitterly. It would probably be glorious tomorrow when they left, and she hadn't been out without an anorak the whole week.

Leaving the dishes to drain, she opened the door and sat on the step, letting the weak sunshine warm her face and thinking that at least when she got home she would be able to wash her hair. It had been too cold and wet until now for her to face the prospect of drying it, though there had certainly been time enough. It had been a wretchedly miserable week. After Mandy deserted her so eagerly each morning she had hardly anything to do except watch the rain or try to read in an attempt to shut Warwick from her mind.

She felt tears welling from her closed lids. God, she seemed to do nothing but cry nowadays! She was run down because she wasn't eating enough. All her clothes were loose, and this morning she had turned away from the reflection of her thin face and unwashed hair in the mirror.

She shivered as the sun was obscured, but it was too much trouble to move and she only leaned her head against the door frame. Then something, some prickling awareness made her open her eyes and she saw Warwick staring down at her.

In sudden, violent anger, he burst out, 'My God, he must have had something to get to you!'

'Yes,' she said flatly.

Standing up, she went inside and Warwick followed, ducking his head in the doorway. She wondered why she was so unsurprised by his appearance, and merely asked, 'How did you find me here?'

'One of your neighbours,' he said briefly.

Lauren nodded. Ann had taken Sarah away for a few days and anyway she wouldn't give her address to Warwick, but she had sent a postcard with a view of the site to one of the upstairs tenants. She remembered now that it had the address printed on the back.

'What do you want?' she said at last.

He flung himself down on the seat opposite. He was too big for it—too big for the whole caravan and ridiculously out of place. He stared at her broodingly, then said, 'God knows. Perhaps I had to come to convince myself of what I saw. I don't know.' He closed his eyes and leaned his head back for a moment, then opened them and let his gaze drift over her. 'You weren't married to him—her father.'

It was a statement rather than a question, but she shook her head.

'What's her name?'

'Amanda—Mandy.'

She looked up and met his eyes. They were blazing, and with a sense of shock she recognised hatred. Not for herself, but for Mandy.

Last week she had tried once more to get Mandy to tell her why she had been so frightened by Warwick, but her carefully worded question had provoked such a frenzied reaction that she had left it. Looking at Warwick now, she remembered her screaming, 'I hate him! He's horrible!' It was ironic that the two people she most loved in the world should react so intensely to each other.

Wearily, she said, 'Why are you asking, Warwick? What does it matter?'

'I'm trying to build up a new picture,' he told her harshly. 'A true one in place of the one you fed me before. Don't you think I've a right to it?'

Shrinking at his tone, she said in feeble defence, 'I warned you I was an illusion.'

He erupted from his seat before she could move. Seizing her hair, he snatched her face round towards him, and with his voice cracking with rage, ordered, 'Don't you dare get flip with me! I had a right to know! Why *didn't* you tell me?'

Lauren could feel the fury in his trembling hands and she held herself rigidly still, afraid to move or speak in case she incited a further outbreak of violence. Her heart thundering, she stared up at him, and he yanked on her hair again. *'Why didn't you tell me?'*

Towering over her, his expression was murderous, his face dark with the fight for control. The hand holding her hair twitched and he brought the other one up to her throat in a painful grip. Between his teeth he muttered, 'I could kill you!'

She believed him, but suddenly she didn't care. Jerking back, she cried vehemently, 'You have *no* rights!'

For a second his grip on her neck tightened, then he slowly released her. 'No,' he agreed bleakly. 'Apparently not even those of common humanity.'

She collapsed back against the seat, rubbing her throat where his fingers had bitten in. It felt bruised and sore, and when she said, 'What do you mean?' it came out as a whisper.

He regarded her in cold contempt. 'To quote you, why are you asking? What does it matter?'

She shook her head, bewildered, and, his voice curt, he asked, 'Why didn't you marry him?'

'A very simple reason.' She got up and poured herself a drink of water to ease her throat, then turned to face him defiantly. 'He wouldn't marry *me*.'

He looked across at her incredulously. 'And you're still in love with a man like that after five—six years?'

His tone was blank with disbelief, and she suddenly laughed because the idea was so ridiculous. His face hardened again. 'The intrepid sailor, I presume. Does he have a wife in every port?'

'No.' She could feel the hysterical laughter welling up in her again and she tried to choke it back. Warwick was watching her intently, his body unnaturally still, and she said flippantly, 'Just the one. He got married a couple of weeks ago.'

'I see.' His gaze slid over her, taking in the hollow cheeks and the straggling hair that he had never before seen anything but shining and clean.

He didn't see, but it was better to let him go on believing what he did. Averting her eyes, Lauren looked through the window and saw he had left the Porsche with a total disregard for the signs indicating where visitors might and might not park.

It was attracting attention, and she said, 'I think you ought to know there's a crowd of small boys round your car, and some of them aren't above carving their initials on the paintwork.'

'Dismissal?' he enquired caustically.

'Is there anything else to say?'

'Only this.'

He leaned forward swiftly to grasp her hands and pull her upright, and uncaring of who might be looking in, kissed her with a savage ferocity that crushed her lips back against her teeth. The embrace was brutal, filled with rage and something that was almost despair. When he released her she staggered back, gasping, and without looking at her he pushed past to the doorway. She thought he was going straight out without a backward glance, but at the last second he paused and looked back.

'When you asked if I had intended to ask you to marry me it was the wrong question.' He had one foot on the ground, his body twisted towards her so that their eyes were on a level. 'The real question was whether I meant it.'

Lauren's breath caught in her throat, and he said derisively, 'But you knew the answer to that one as well, didn't you?'

He turned away, finally this time, and Lauren watched him stride to the Porsche and scatter the boys who were bouncing on the bumper, uttering some sharp command that made them fall back. He swept the car in a tight circle, then he was hidden from her behind the serried rows of caravans.

Pain seized in her chest, constricting her breathing. No, she hadn't needed to ask, but Warwick's oblique confirmation only worsened the agony. She sat for a long time, then glanced dully at her watch. Mandy had been driven from her mind, but now she realised she was late coming back. Her taut nerves jumping, she wondered if she had come when Warwick was there, and went cold at the thought. It would be impossible to make a child who had witnessed that burst of violence believe that such things could happen because of frustrated love.

Mandy hadn't seen Warwick, but she had seen and recognised the car. Lauren found her being fussed over by Ben's parents, and literally dragged her, screaming, to their own van. Too strained and mentally exhausted to display sympathy, she dumped her roughly on the long seat and applied a cold, wet flannel to her streaming eyes. Mandy's crying ceased abruptly, and Lauren said forcefully, 'You can just stop it or I'll really give you something to cry about! You're being completely silly! You don't know this man or anything about him. You've never even spoken to him, so why are you making all this ridiculous fuss?'

'I want my real daddy,' Mandy declared. 'I won't have him instead of my real daddy!'

Lauren stared at her, astounded. 'What on earth are you talking about? And don't start to cry again,' she added hastily. 'I warn you I'm not in the mood for it!'

Mandy gulped. 'I don't want to have a stepdaddy. Stepdaddies are horrible!'

'Who told you that?' Lauren demanded, beginning to have an inkling.

'Melissa at school. She's got one and she hates him. He's cruel to her.'

'And Melissa's the biggest story-teller I've ever come across,' Lauren said roundly, her lips tightening as she remembered the shy, gentle man she had met at parents' evenings at the school. 'I'm going to have a few words with her mother, but in the meantime you can just tell me what she's been saying.'

It all came pouring out then. Lauren didn't know

whether to be appalled or to admire such in-
ventiveness. The brothers Grimm had nothing on one
small seven-year-old with a gullible audience, she
realised, listening to horrifying tales of starvation and
beatings.

When Mandy had finished she said, 'I've never heard
such fairy tales in the whole of my life! I would have
thought you had more sense than to believe such fibs!
What on earth would her mummy be doing to let such
things happen?'

'Her mummy doesn't want her any more now she's
got a new daddy,' said Mandy, but in a small voice and
with less conviction.

'Don't be silly! Though I shouldn't be surprised if she
gets her bottom smacked occasionally for going round
telling stories like that about her new daddy.'

'She wants her real daddy back.'

'Yes,' said Lauren, feeling a sadness in spite of herself
for a child who couldn't understand why such things
happened in the adult world around her. She could
imagine the jealousy and insecurity which had
prompted Melissa to weave her tales.

'He will come back,' Mandy said with a return of
obstinacy. 'He told her so.'

'No, darling,' Lauren insisted more gently. 'He'll
probably see her quite often, and she might go to stay
with him sometimes, but he won't come back.'

'He will, he will!' Mandy's voice rose. 'Real daddies
always come back, and mine will as well!'

With a sudden coldness Lauren wondered how long
she had been consoling herself with her fantasy. No
wonder she had reacted so violently to Warwick! With
the image of stepfathers implanted by Melissa he would
be a frightening figure, filling her with terror on the one
hand and threatening her dream on the other.

She looked down to find Mandy's eyes fixed on her

hopefully. 'You told me he was nice,' she said. 'I asked you and you told me.'

'Yes, but . . .' Helplessly, Lauren took a deep breath. 'I'm sorry, darling, but he won't come back. He's married another lady, you see, and gone to live a long, long way away.'

At first Mandy wouldn't believe her, clinging desperately to her illusion and refusing to heed any words which might shatter it. She stormed and wept, but finally subsided into hiccupping calm and asked, 'How do you know he's married another lady?'

'Because his mummy wrote to me and told me about it. Here!' Lauren reached into her bag for the letter and took it out of the envelope. 'It says so on the second page.' She held it up for Mandy's inspection, knowing she wouldn't be able to read Mrs Munro's crabbed writing.

'Which line does it say so on?'

'That one and that one and that one.' Lauren moved her finger along as she spoke, and convinced, Mandy's shoulders drooped. Lauren dropped the letter on the seat and put her arms round her. 'Never mind,' she whispered. 'You've got me and I love you.'

'Lots and lots and for ever?' Mandy queried.

'Lots and lots and for ever,' Lauren confirmed gravely. 'Though this last week I'd begun to wonder if a certain little girl still loved her mummy.'

Mandy squirmed round to clutch her, the unspoken reply more vivid than words. Lauren rocked her gently for a while, then Mandy stirred and said, 'And that man isn't going to be my stepdaddy?'

'No,' said Lauren.

A spasm crossed her features for a second, and Mandy asked, 'What's the matter? Your face went funny.'

Lauren smiled. 'I've got a bit of a headache.'

She had been aware of it since Warwick left, and the

scene when she dragged Mandy back hadn't improved
it. Tension, she thought, and perhaps having her hair
yanked as well. Warwick hadn't been gentle.

She saw Ben approaching the caravan and when she
opened the door he said, 'Me mum says can Ginger
come to tea.'

All the trauma forgotten, Mandy slid off the seat to
join him and they went off together, arguing before they
had gone more than a few yards. Wearily, Lauren
leaned back, feeling her head begin to throb in earnest.
She would pack tomorrow, she decided. She would
have time, and at the moment she felt almost ill. For
once in her life she felt she could do with a drink. She
thought of all the money Mandy had fed into slot
machines during the last week. She hadn't spent a
penny on herself so far, and with sudden resolution she
went up to the supermarket and bought herself half a
bottle of cheap Spanish wine.

It was so innocuous it tasted like grape cordial, and a
second glass did nothing to ease either her headache or
her depression. When her vision began to be obscured
by zigzag flashes of light she realised it wasn't going to.
A migraine was all she needed to complete a perfect
day—a perfect week, for that matter.

She drew the curtains to shut out the sunlight and lay
down, but the pain got worse and eventually she
acknowledged that she would have to take the tablets
she had been prescribed. They made her feel drugged
and confused and she avoided them if she could, but
her head had reached the stage where it was the lesser
of two evils.

Groaning, she pulled the seat out into a bed and
fetched a glass of water. The dose was two, but the
chemist had told her she could take three as long as she
didn't make a habit of it. She shrugged and emptied
two into her palm, fastening the child-proof stopper

carefully and lying back down with the bottle still in her hand.

For a while she drifted, unable to sleep properly because the pain was so severe, and after a while she struggled to a sitting position again. It was becoming unendurable. The chemist had said she was allowed to take three. She swallowed them dry, washing them down with water afterwards.

By now she felt sick and the fingers of her right hand were beginning to go numb. She looked down at them, barely able to see for the flashes of light in front of her. She knew she hadn't put the cap back on the bottle and she must, because of Mandy. But her fingers would no longer perform the task and she tried with her left hand, giving a sob of frustration when the rest of the tablets spilled out on the bed.

She tried to gather them up again, dropping as many as she collected. Confused, and desperate to keep them out of Mandy's reach, she put some in her mouth and some in the bottle, and when she could find no more she closed her eyes and tightened her hand over the container.

CHAPTER NINE

OCCASIONALLY Lauren heard voices, but they receded again before she could answer them. One voice in particular troubled her, the deep tones sometimes coaxing, sometimes goading, so that she wanted to tell it to stop. But her tongue was so thick and slow in her mouth that it wouldn't form the words, and she would drift into darkness again because it was too much trouble to try.

But still the voice went on, pulling at her, forcing her to make some response, and eventually she opened her eyes.

'Come on—come *on*!' Warwick said urgently. 'What sort of a mother are you, for God's sake?'

He was holding her hand in both of his, and as he read the recognition in her eyes, his grip tightened until her fingers felt crushed. When she made a small sound of protest he grimaced, realising what he had been doing, and his hold was relaxed though he did not release her.

Lauren stared round her, the small bare room confirming what the smell of antiseptic had told her even in her half conscious state.

'Mandy,' she whispered. 'Where is she?'

'She's all right,' Warwick told her. 'Rachel's looking after her.'

She couldn't think who Rachel was, but the calm reassurance of his reply dulled her anxiety and her eyes gradually closed again. When she woke the next time a blue-uniformed nurse was sitting watching her. She tried to pull herself up in the bed and the nurse said, 'Don't move your arm. You're on a drip.'

158

Lauren turned her head and saw that her arm was bandaged to a rail on the bed to keep it immobile, and she was attached by a tube to the bottle above.

'I'll tell Sister you're awake,' the nurse said. 'You may be able to come off it now.'

A doctor came in with the Sister. His tone was professional, and though he asked how she felt he seemed as impersonal as the nurse. They came later and dismantled the drip, and it wasn't until she was alone again that Lauren realised she still hadn't asked them what was the matter with her.

She was thirstily swallowing the water in her glass when Warwick came. He stood for a moment by the door looking at her, then crossed the room to drop into the bedside chair. His attitude was weary and distant, and she said hesitantly, 'Warwick . . .?'

There were so many things she wanted to ask him—why she was here, when she could see Mandy—but his expression of frowning discouragement was making it difficult. Again, she said, 'Warwick . . .?' and he turned his head quickly, his eyes suddenly blazing.

'Why did you do it?' he demanded harshly. 'God knows you had me completely fooled, but I still wouldn't have put you down as a coward!'

Bewildered, she said weakly, 'I don't know what you mean. What are you talking about?'

'What the hell do you think I'm talking about!' he returned savagely.

She closed her eyes for a moment, retreating from his anger. 'Please, Warwick! I shouldn't be asking if I knew.'

'Do you mean you really don't know why you're here?'

She met his sceptical gaze and shook her head. 'No. No one told me.' She gave a feeble smile. 'And when I began to wonder there was no one here to ask.'

He let out his breath in a sigh, leaning his head back on the chair, then asked, 'What's the last thing you remember?'

Lauren searched back. Her recollections were woolly and clouded, and it took a long time to sort them and put them in order in her mind. Eventually, she said slowly, 'I had a migraine and I took my tablets . . .'

'Yes!' Warwick interrupted, his voice savage again. 'You did! nearly a whole bloody bottle full!'

'No!' she whispered, stunned.

'Yes!' He made the contradiction grimly, then went on, 'On top of nearly half a bottle of wine, when it's written in large red letters straight across the top of the label that in no circumstances are they to be taken in conjunction with alcohol!'

Appalled, she realised what he said was true. She had read the instructions when she first had the tablets, but the warning had left no impression because normally she never drank. She hadn't even glanced at them since.

'I'd forgotten,' she told him, still whispering. 'I never drink at home and I'd forgotten. Did you think . . .'

The question tailed away. Of course he did. And the doctor and the nurses and everyone else. But it hurt that Warwick believed it, no matter how damning the evidence.

'I would never do such a thing!' she protested. 'Never! What would happen to Mandy? How could you think I would?'

He got up and walked restlessly to the window and back again. 'Until a week ago I didn't even know she existed, so how could I know how much you cared for her?'

The reply silenced her for a moment, then she asked, 'How is she?'

'Distressed. What would you expect?' he said curtly. Glancing down at her suddenly white face, he relented.

'The boys and Karen are helping to take her mind off it and she'll be all right once she's seen you. I'll bring her tomorrow.'

'Thank you. Did . . .' Lauren swallowed, then went on again, 'Did she find me?'

'Yes,' he said in the same brusque tones. He squared his shoulders. 'I found her trying to wake you, but she hadn't realised there was anything wrong. She didn't have the shock that I did.'

'I'm sorry.' The phrase seemed so inadequate she didn't know why she had said it. 'Did you bring me here?'

'Yes,' he said again. He turned away from her and stared out of the window. 'I remembered passing the hospital on the way to the caravan site, so I just grabbed you and Mandy and that bloody bottle and drove here with my hand on the horn.' His voice unnaturally flat, he continued, 'We didn't know how many tablets were in the bottle in the first place, so we couldn't tell how many you'd taken. They got a stomach pump on you right away, but apparently when they're mixed with alcohol quite a small number can be lethal.'

He swung round again, and Lauren saw that his forehead and top lip were glistening with sweat. Violently, he said, 'You bloody little fool! Don't you know you could just as easily have been brain-damaged? A cabbage for life?'

'It wasn't intentional, Warwick,' she protested pleadingly.

His lips twisted. 'Just a cry for help.'

Wearily, she said, 'All right, don't believe me. There's no way I can make you.'

He didn't reply and she looked round the room. 'This is a private ward, isn't it? You must be paying.'

'We'll sort it out later,' he told her briefly.

'How long have I been here?'

'Three days,' he said. 'I collected all your stuff out of the caravan and took it down to Rachel's place with Mandy.'

'Thank you,' she said stiltedly. 'It was good of you to look after Mandy. I'm very grateful. And to Rachel, of course.'

'Oh, for God's sake,' he said impatiently. 'How many people *would* abandon a crying six-year-old! I admit I didn't know what to do with her in the beginning—I took her to the flat expecting Ann to be there, but she wasn't, and nobody could tell me where to find her. Mandy said she'd stayed with Sarah's grandparents the other week and that raised my hopes for a while, but unfortunately she was vague about the address and we couldn't reach agreement on a surname.'

'It's Braithwaite,' Lauren told him. 'She can't pronounce it.'

For a moment he smiled, saying drily, 'That explains it,' then the smile faded. Thrusting his hands into his pockets, he said, 'Anyway, I couldn't think of anywhere else, so I took her to Rachel.'

'I'm sorry,' Lauren said helplessly. 'I've caused a lot of trouble.'

'It's been an eventful few days,' he agreed. 'Especially as I'm without a secretary.' When she was silent, he queried, 'Am I?'

'I don't know,' she said in a low voice. To her relief Warwick made no further comment, and to change the subject she asked, 'Have they told you when I can leave here? They don't talk to me a great deal.'

'In a day or two, as long as you have someone to look after you.' His tone expressionless, he added, 'The doctor in charge wants you to see a psychiatrist first.'

Lauren flushed hotly. 'I don't need one! I keep telling

you it was an accident, and I'm certainly never likely to do anything so stupid again!'

'All right, I'll tell him.' He pressed her hand, impersonally and briefly. 'I'll bring Mandy to see you tomorrow.'

'Thank you.' Her eyes blurred so much that she didn't see him leave, and heedlessly she let the tears run down her cheeks. The nurse came in and tut-tutted, and for the first time there was a slight unbending in her manner. Rearranging the pillows, she said, 'Come on, this won't do. You mustn't start getting depressed again.'

'I am *not* depressed!' Lauren shouted, in the sudden rage of weakness. She saw the nurse look startled, and sniffed, reaching for a tissue from the locker. 'I'm sorry,' she apologised. 'Perhaps I *am* a bit down, but I'm definitely not suicidal. My trouble is that I don't read labels on bottles and I forgot I wasn't supposed to take my tablets on top of alcohol. I don't drink either, so it hadn't registered. A couple of sherries at Christmas is the sum total in most years.'

The nurse still betrayed faint doubt as she took her pulse and blood pressure, but Lauren sensed that on the whole she was believed. She said, 'Then make sure you read them in future. You were lucky this time.'

She filled in the chart and hung it back on the rail at the foot of the bed. 'You gave Mr Sinclair rather a fright. He didn't leave the hospital the first two nights.'

'Didn't he?' Lauren returned listlessly. 'He's been very good.' The nurse raised her eyebrows slightly at her lack of interest, and she added, 'He's my boss.'

The nurse smiled significantly, but she only said, 'I wish he was mine,' before rustling out again.

Lauren was told the next morning that she could go on to a light diet, and though she wasn't hungry she forced the food down, alarmed by the sight of her white, wasted legs. In the mirror above the washbasin her face was even worse, her eyes huge, with unhealthy, brown-shadowed lids, and her hair looked and felt disgusting.

She bought some shampoo and a newspaper from the trolley, but she couldn't even make the effort to read the paper properly. Only the day and date on the front held her attention. Tuesday! There were three days of her life she would never remember. She went cold as she realised she could so easily have lost all memory for ever.

She was folding the paper when it struck her that Warwick should have been in Paris to discuss the Rouillière contract. Jerkily she unfolded the paper and checked the date again. The twenty-seventh, and she had booked the hotel herself for three days commencing the twenty-sixth.

By visiting time she was sick with guilt and tension, and Warwick and Mandy were late. She could hear all the other visitors arriving, and lay back against her banked pillows imagining all the disasters which could have prevented their coming. When her door was pushed open at last and she saw Mandy standing there, relief made her speechless. Small and overawed by her surroundings, Mandy fixed her eyes on her fearfully. She seemed rooted to the spot, as though everything was too much for her, and Warwick gave her a gentle shove, saying, 'Go on, moppet! Say hello!'

Mandy flung herself into Lauren's outstretched arms, clutching her with such silent feeling that Lauren felt the ever-ready tears come to her eyes again.

'You've woken up,' Mandy said at last. 'I shook you and shook you in the caravan, but you wouldn't wake up.'

'I know, darling,' Lauren murmured. 'I wasn't well then, but I'm better now.'

'Properly better?'

'Almost. I shall be in a few days.' Lauren rubbed the top of Mandy's head with her chin and looked up to find Warwick watching them with a faint smile.

He went to her washbasin and began to scrub his hands, then said, 'I'm sorry we were late, but I had to change a wheel.'

'It was on the motorway,' Mandy confirmed importantly. 'And Uncle Rick said a bad word that the boys say in the playground at school.'

'I told you not to tell anyone about that, you little madam,' he said goodhumouredly.

'Oh.' She looked at him, crestfallen in case he was displeased. 'I thought you just meant that I wasn't to say what the word was.'

Bouncing experimentally on the bed, she turned back to Lauren. 'Uncle Rick says you're coming back with us when you're better. Are you sure you aren't better today?'

'No, she isn't,' Warwick told her. 'And you'll have the nurses after you if you jump on the bed! It isn't allowed.'

Mandy grinned at him mischievously, and Lauren had to swallow a lump in her throat before she could speak. Feeling his eyes on her, she said, 'I can't come back with you, Warwick.'

'You're not going anywhere else.' The smile was still there for Mandy's benefit, but his voice was inflexible. 'You can come out tomorrow as long as you get proper care. Going back to that damp bedroom and looking after Mandy doesn't come under that heading, and you would find anyway that it was beyond you.'

'Ann would help.'

'She still isn't back. I've been trying to get her since Friday to let her know what had happened, and I rang again before I started out this morning. Besides,

Rachel's expecting you. She made the offer—I didn't ask her to take you, and you needn't worry, I shan't be there much myself. I've got a pile of work and I can't afford the time.'

'All right,' said Lauren in a subdued voice. 'I didn't mean to sound ungrateful.' She shrank from facing them, particularly James, but she would have to see them anyway to thank them for taking Mandy in, and it didn't sound as though Rachel was hostile. After a pause, she asked, 'Warwick, what about the Rouillière contract? You're supposed to be over there.'

Indifferently, he said, 'If I lose it, I lose it. It was between three of us, so there's no guarantee I'd get it anyway.'

Lauren thought of the weeks of work he and all the others had put into preparing the quote. All wasted effort because of her crass stupidity—a stupidity Warwick wouldn't believe, though it wasn't really so surprising. Only a few hours before she took the overdose she had deliberately allowed him to believe she was still in love with Trevor. It had seemed for the best, but her accident had changed everything and her indebtedness was getting deeper and deeper—the cost of her treatment here, the Rouillière contract, almost certainly her life. If Warwick hadn't found her it could have been too late before Mandy became sufficiently worried to call anyone to her. It would have been the mad drive to the hospital which frightened her and made her realise something was desperately wrong.

How could she repay him for her life? Only with herself, and now it seemed he no longer wanted her.

The bell in the corridor signalled the end of visiting time, and Warwick said, 'I'll get Rachel to put your clothes in a case for tomorrow. Is there anything else you need?'

When she shook her head he ruffled Mandy's hair.

'Come on then, moppet. Let's go before we're thrown out.'

Mandy kissed her goodbye, holding her breath to make it last as long as possible. Her lips were faintly sticky and smelled of peppermint, and with a rush of love, Lauren hugged her fiercely and possessively. Only as she reluctantly released her did she become aware of Warwick's cynical gaze, and she felt herself flush.

He said, 'I'll try to get here about twelve, but don't hold me to it. I've got a meeting which might stretch on a bit.'

She nodded, trying to push down the hurt at his words. He might have been talking to a business colleague from his tone, and he had stayed on the far side of the room for the whole of the brief visit. He hadn't even bothered to hide the fact that he was anxious to get away. Visitors usually hung on for as long as they could—she'd heard the nurses going along the corridor ejecting them, but Warwick had begun his departure the moment the bell went.

She said, 'Thank you, I'll be as ready as I can,' and he stood with one hand on the door, suppressed impatience in every line of his body as Mandy kissed her goodbye again.

Time passed with excruciating slowness when they had gone and she lay awake half the night. In the morning the doctor came to see her for the last time, critical because she still refused to see the psychiatrist, then she washed her hair in the bath and collected her things together on the bed.

A nurse at last brought the case with her clothes and told her Warwick was in the waiting room downstairs. When she was dressed she went to the staff room at the end of the corridor and thanked the other nurses for their care, but the smiles she got in response were stiff and forced, making her wish she hadn't gone.

Just as her own was, she thought, as she greeted Warwick. He scanned her face quickly and asked, 'Are you sure you can walk to the car park? We can get a wheelchair.'

Hoping it was true, she said, 'I can manage,' and slid her hand through the arm he offered.

It took all her will power to make the distance, and Warwick had to hold her up for the last few yards. The feel of his arms about her brought on a wild yearning, but it seemed that what she was now so willing to give he no longer desired. Whatever he felt for her she had effectively killed.

She didn't blame him. From his viewpoint he would be a fool to come back for more after all the separate blows she had dealt him, and the time was past for explanations. After a deception of such magnitude, whatever she told him he would doubt.

The drive tired her more than she would have believed possible and she swayed as she got out of the car. Warwick helped her inside and said, 'I think you'd better go straight to bed. Mandy and everyone else can come and see you there.'

Feeling as she did she had no wish to argue, but looking up the long flight of stairs she wondered if she could manage them. Warwick saw her unexpressed doubt, and with an exclamation he swung her into his arms and carried her up. She lay limply against him, aware of the thud of his heart even though he held her as though she were weightless. Probably to him she was. There had never been much of her anyway, and now there was even less.

In the bedroom he set her on her feet and studied her face. Momentarily, his own showed concern as he said, 'Can you manage? I can send Rachel or Mrs Penkridge up to you.'

'I'm all right. I've only got to get out of my clothes.'

He smiled, a savage expression without kindness or humour. 'I won't offer to help you myself,' he told her, and Lauren closed her eyes for a second, to find when she opened them that he had left her so abruptly she was staring at the closing door.

The housekeeper brought up her small suitcase and Lauren extracted her nightdress and got into bed. Rachel came up afterwards, hand in hand with Mandy and bearing a small radio.

'The boys and Karen wanted to come as well,' she said, 'but I suspect their motives weren't so much sympathetic as morbidly curious.' The dark eyes, so very much like Warwick's, creased in amusement. 'But Mandy's been very good, haven't you, moppet?'

'Yes,' Mandy agreed. 'Auntie Rachel says I'm a good girl because I eat all my cabbage and Mike and Howard won't.'

'That's no particular virtue,' said Lauren, laughing. 'You like cabbage.'

'I know, but I eat my green beans as well and I *don't* like those.' She slid her sandals off and climbed on to the cover beside Lauren. 'Do you still have to stop in bed all the time?'

'No,' Lauren said. 'I was a bit tired because I've come a long way in the car, but I'll get up again at tea time.'

Mandy wriggled restlessly, too full of energy to lie still once she was assured that Lauren was no longer really ill. 'I like it here. They've got two dogs and a *huge* big garden and fields with horses in them. When I went out to play in the garden, Karen had to come with me at first to make sure I didn't get lost.' She propelled herself backwards on to the floor and pushed her feet back into her sandals. 'Karen's waiting for me to go and play with her.'

'You go along, then,' said Lauren. 'I'm going to have a little sleep in a minute.'

She watched Mandy go, then met Rachel's eyes and said simply, 'Thank you for all you've done. It sounds inadequate, but you know how I feel. You must have had quite a bit of trouble with her.'

'A few problems to start with,' Rachel admitted. 'I'm telling you because you would find out anyway. Apparently she was frantic at first—she thought Warwick was kidnapping you both, then when you were whistled off with such speed at the hospital she picked up the urgency and realised you were in danger.' She smiled. 'Afterwards, when the panic was over, she recovered with unflattering ease, but you may have a few repercussions. She had quite a shock.' She paused and said deliberately, 'So did Rick.'

Her tone was cooler, and Lauren said quickly, 'It was an accident, Rachel, I swear!' Her eyes clouded. 'Warwick doesn't believe me, I know, but it's true.' Sighing, she added, 'I suppose it's hard to swallow. I've read in the papers about people taking accidental overdoses and I've never understood how it could happen. It seems so impossible, but believe me, it isn't. I remember taking those first two tablets and then deciding to have one more, but the rest is a complete blank. I've no memory at all of taking the others. I certainly didn't intend to.' With a burst of irritation she added, 'And I don't know what reason I'm supposed to have for intending to either!'

Looking up, she caught a fleeting relief in Rachel's expression and was suddenly struck by its cause. Shaken, she exclaimed, 'You thought it was because of Warwick!'

Faintly uncomfortable, Rachel said, 'I knew the course of true love had hit an almighty obstacle. When I asked Rick why you could have done it, he told me to mind my own bloody business. He tends to be outspoken, but he's not usually quite so rude. Not with me at least.'

She wandered across the room and stood looking out over the garden. The sounds of children's voices and barking dogs floated in through the window, and she smiled at what she saw, then turned back, her face serious again.

'You and Rick did such a convincing job on Tessa that you rather convinced me as well. Even James thought he detected a practice ring on the wedding bells, but when he sounded him out a few days later, Rick bit his head off.' Surveying Lauren, she said calmly, 'You did have rather a large skeleton in your cupboard, didn't you? And I suspect that the door fell open and revealed it accidentally.'

'Yes,' Lauren agreed wearily. 'I thought Warwick wanted an affair, and I wasn't willing. In the beginning there were reasons against telling him about Mandy, and I kept it from everyone at work, not just him.' Half pleadingly, she said, 'You must know what he's like, Rachel. It never occurred to me for a moment that he might be serious.' She coloured under Rachel's steady regard, and went on, 'I was going to tell him once the dinner was over, but there was a—misunderstanding— before I got the chance.'

Rachel paused, considering, then asked abruptly, 'Do you love him?'

There was no point in denying it, and in a low voice Lauren said, 'Yes.'

'And you've now reached an impasse,' Rachel commented. She sat on the end of the bed and studied Lauren appraisingly for a moment. 'I don't know what the solution is, and I imagine there's more to it than you've told me. The only suggestion I've got to make is that you try going to bed with him—you'd be no worse off than you are now, and it sometimes sorts things out. I'd do it fairly quickly as well—once you leave here you may find it's out of your hands.'

Lauren tried to swallow the constriction in her throat and said dully, 'I think it's already too late. He's not interested now.'

Rachel shrugged. 'Taking it all round you can't be surprised if he appears to have turned against you, but I think he's covering, and he'll go on covering unless you make a move. It's your turn now, and to be blunt, I think you owe it to him.' She grinned suddenly. 'And yes, I do know what he's like, so he shouldn't be too difficult to seduce!'

As the week progressed, Lauren thought despairingly that if he was covering, he was doing it very well. She saw him only twice and on both occasions she wouldn't even have known he was in the house if it had been left to him. The first time she heard Mandy's squeal of greeting and came in from the garden to find him swinging her into the air. Just outside the French windows she halted, wishing with anguish that he would treat her to the same unshadowed smile, and waiting for his features to harden when he caught sight of her.

The expression faded as she knew it would, and setting Mandy down on her feet, he said, 'Hello. You're looking better.'

Stiltedly, to cover her hurt, she replied, 'That isn't much of a compliment. I could hardly look worse than the last time you saw me.'

'I was expressing an opinion on your apparent state of health,' Warwick said evenly.

She knew he was, but she had dressed and made up with care each day, deliberately leaving her hair loose the way he liked it. She had hoped for something, even if it was only the faintest echo of what used to be in his eyes when he looked at her.

'Could I talk to you some time?' she asked.

'Yes, but I'm afraid not now. I've only called in for some papers James left for me.'

Within five minutes he had left again, and the next time she didn't even see him, only heard his voice from the other side of the study door as he and James argued amicably over something.

Tartly, she asked Rachel if she would try to make an appointment for her as she would like to discuss her future with him, and she suspected the message had been delivered verbatim when Warwick rang her from Fenmore's.

'Is it urgent?' he asked.

He was using his clipped, office voice, and she made her own equally cool. 'It's becoming urgent. I'm perfectly well now and I must make some decisions on what I'm going to do. Mandy should be at school—the new term has already started.'

'Very well,' he said. 'I'll come down this evening, though I may be late. Tell Rachel I shall already have eaten.'

The phone was replaced before she even had time to say goodbye, and Rachel pulled a wry face when she reported the brief conversation. 'He really is becoming very uncommunicative,' she observed. 'I did try to talk to him about you myself.'

'What happened?'

'He listened,' Rachel said. 'Politely.'

Dispirited, Lauren tried to marshall her thoughts as she waited for him that evening. Rachel and James had gone to the theatre, whether fortunately or unfortunately she didn't know, and it was the housekeeper's weekend off. Just before she went, Rachel had poured a large measure of sherry which she had put down beside her saying, 'Dutch courage.' At first Lauren only sipped it, but as the evening wore on her nervousness increased and she got up and refilled the glass.

The two labradors lifted their heads when Warwick arrived, though she hadn't heard him herself. He greeted them first, and in fairness she admitted he didn't have much option. 'I should learn from them,' she thought, watching the dogs push their noses under his hand. 'Animals don't suffer from inhibitions— they're not afraid to make the initial approach.'

Warwick straightened from patting them and looked round. As though surprised to find her alone, he asked, 'Where's Rachel?'

'She's gone to the theatre with James.'

A flicker of something showed in his eyes and without moving he seemed to distance himself from her still further. He poured himself a Scotch and Lauren offered to fetch some ice, but he shook his head indifferently. 'I'll just have water with it.'

He lowered himself into the chair opposite as he spoke, and summoning her courage she said hesitantly, 'You mentioned once about me coming back to work for you.'

She let the question show in her tone, and staring beyond her, he took a mouthful from his glass. 'Yes, I've been thinking about it. On reflection it's perhaps not such a good idea.'

'Are you replacing with me with a word processor, or did the typing pool yield something worthwhile?' she enquired acidly. She doubted whether she could really have brought herself to go back, but his decision stung, nevertheless.

Without meeting her eyes he put his glass down on the floor beside him and said tonelessly, 'Why should you care?'

If only she'd had the simple outlook of the labrador at his feet she could have told him. Silently, within her, she cried, 'Because I love you and because I shall never feel for anyone else what I feel for you.'

Aloud, she said, 'A perverted sense of duty, obviously.'

He ignored the bite in her words. 'I'll send you your maximum sick pay—that should give you a reasonable opportunity to find another job.' He read her instinctive denial and exclaimed tautly, 'Oh, don't bother to argue! I'll re-phrase it. Fenmore's, the company which employs you and of which I happen to be chairman will send you your sick pay. Personalities are actually irrelevant.'

Lauren bowed her head, knowing she couldn't afford pride. Distantly, she said, 'I should like to know how much my hospital bill was as well, please.'

'Forget it,' he returned shortly. Standing up, he removed his jacket and flung it over the back of the chair, then met her obstinate stare. 'Whatever you say I shan't tell you. If I take something on without consulting the person concerned, I automatically discharge it.'

She was silent, knowing it was useless to force the issue, and he asked abruptly, 'Have you seen a doctor since you've been here?'

'No. Why should I?'

His eyes scrutinised her, taking in her pallor and tight expression. 'You're depressed. You should get something for it.'

'Oh, for God's sake!' she burst out wildly. 'I'm afraid now to take a damned aspirin for a headache! The last thing I need is more tablets!'

'Perhaps if you'd got help before it would never have happened.' Warwick paused, his eyes flicking over her again. 'You were crying when I came to the caravan that afternoon.'

'Yes.' Tiredly, she defended herself. 'I'd had a bad week and I was upset, but that doesn't make me suicidal. Why won't you believe me?'

With sudden harshness, he demanded, 'What else would anyone believe when they find a woman unconscious, clutching a nearly empty bottle of tablets and a letter telling them the father of their child has just married someone else!'

She stared at him incredulously, and he said, 'You can't deny what I found.'

She couldn't. She remembered dropping the letter back on the seat after showing it to Mandy, and it was quite possible it had been under her hand. With that shattering migraine she hadn't been in a state to notice anything.

'No,' she told him. 'I can't deny what you found, but I deny your conclusions!' Distinctly and emphatically, she went on, 'I don't give a damn who Trevor marries! If he drove his car off the top of a Scottish mountain I wouldn't even send a wreath to his funeral!'

For a moment Warwick's face was stunned, then it twisted in cynicism. 'A man you made love with? *You?*' he shook his head slowly. 'You've got to have been in love with him, so don't give me that! I'd lay the last penny I possess that I'm the only other man ever to get near you. And then only under the demoralising influence of alcohol,' he finished bleakly.

Her bitterness spilling over, she said, 'You're so right! But it obviously hasn't occurred to you that it might be because it was an experience I didn't want repeated!'

'What?' His eyes lifted to her face, suddenly alert. 'What do you mean?'

Dully, she said, 'He forced me.'

'Raped you?'

His face was ferocious in its blending of shock and rage as she nodded. She saw his hands clench on the arms of the chair until the knuckles were bloodless. 'Oh, it wasn't like some stranger pouncing on me in the dark,' she said, her voice colourless. 'I was going out with him. At seventeen I even thought I was in love with him, but I wasn't ready for what he wanted. I was partly to blame, I suppose. He used the eternal, "You would if you really cared for me" and he got me nearly there. Perhaps I was stupid in those days, but I didn't realise that by then I didn't have a choice.'

She met Warwick's raw gaze, her own eyes darkened with remembered shame and despair. 'I was incredibly naïve. He said he loved me and I believed him. You don't expect . . .' She hesitated, her voice quivering. 'You don't expect brute force under those circumstances.'

There was a silence, then Warwick rasped, 'And afterwards? When he knew you were pregnant?'

'He skipped,' she said. 'Off to sea in the old traditional manner.'

'God Almighty!' he breathed.

His unfocussed gaze fixed on a point above her head and she knew he was thinking of that high note of revulsion which had broken from her, when for a moment he had used his strength on her, pinning her down when she struggled.

'You couldn't know,' she said, 'but you used almost exactly the same words that he did.'

In the frozen silence she heard the ticking of the clock over the fireplace, and one of the dogs chewing frantically at a sudden, violent itch. Warwick spoke at last, his voice drained. 'But why didn't you tell me? You knew what I thought, what I felt, at the time.'

'What was the point?' she asked listlessly. 'There was still Mandy.'

The insurmountable barrier then as now, she thought, though she didn't put it into words.

She knew she hadn't needed to when Warwick said, 'I see. You were leaving me an escape route.'

'It seemed the easiest solution. You didn't know all the rest. It isn't something I ever tell anyone anyway. I would be too afraid of Mandy somehow getting to hear of it.'

'But when I knew about Mandy—when I came to the caravan! You let me go on believing you were still in love with her father!'

'But nothing had really changed, except that I had a daughter who had hysterics if she so much as saw your car, and you displayed hatred at the mention of her name.'

'Oh, God, it wasn't for *her*!' he exclaimed. 'It was what she represented!—the proof that you'd let another man make love to you when you used to flinch if I even touched you accidentally! And when I thought I'd got you over it at last, you stuck a knife in my guts with a single word!'

He studied her for a moment, his eyes moving over her features and the lines of her cheek and jaw, then said almost painfully, 'How could I hate her? Looking at her face is like looking at yours.'

Lauren smiled, her lips trembling. 'It doesn't seem to have given you much pleasure recently!'

He hesitated, still studying her, then he got up and pulled her back with him on to his own chair. For a long while they lay there, quiet and unmoving, and when Lauren turned her head to speak, he put his finger against her lips.

Because words can mislead, Lauren thought as he kissed her, but this doesn't. This is truth, whatever we say afterwards.

She tried to send him all her emotions through the contact of body and mouth, letting them flow from her and holding nothing back. His hands tightened until the grip was almost painful, then became gentle as they moved to her breasts. When he lifted his head at last she was shaking, and he turned her until her back was resting on his chest, his hands slack on her ribcage.

'I think I should warn you this is imposing a very severe strain on my self-control,' he told her.

The words were muttered, his voice thick and unsteady, then she felt his chest lift in silent laughter, and amusement was woven into the desire in his tones as he added, 'Though you could hardly fail to be aware of it!' The fingers resting on her dug briefly into the flesh over her ribs. 'So before it goes any further, when are you going to marry me?'

During those long moments of quiet before he kissed her, Lauren had reached a decision. She said, 'This year, next year, some time.'

Warwick didn't finish the quote, nor ask her why. In the silence she could feel him thinking, and he said at last, 'So what now?'

In reply she pressed herself deliberately back against him, and he drew in a sudden, sharp breath. Motionless after that one quick movement, he said quietly, 'That can be a very dangerous thing to do unless you mean it.' He paused to allow her to weigh his words. 'Do you?'

He was holding himself rigidly still, and Lauren turned and put her lips against the clenched line of his jaw. When he made no response, she lifted herself until she could reach his mouth, touching him lightly and drawing away, then reaching up to touch again. He didn't return the kisses, instead turning her face so he could look at her, his dark eyes intent.

'Be sure, darling,' he said. 'Be very sure. I'm not going to make love to you for the first time down here, with the dogs round us, and where James and Rachel could walk in saying it was a lousy show and they left in the interval. The first time is going to be in bed where we can lock the door and take it slowly, but to get there we've got to go up those stairs, and there's something about a flight of stairs that has made a lot of women change their minds in the past. Don't back out on me this time.'

Her mouth gone dry, she shook her head. 'I won't.'

He was right about stairs, Lauren found. By the time they reached his room her heated blood had cooled, and Warwick, with a quick, comprehending glance at her, closed the door with his shoulder and slid the bolt home.

Her heart began to pound, nerves and the chill wind of reason warring with love. She stepped back in involuntary retreat as he moved towards her, but his arms captured her and his mouth checked the first words of protest. He kissed her until her body slackened in acceptance, then began to tense again as the movements of his parted lips revived the flickering fire within her. Forced hard against him by the pressure of his hand in the small of her back, she felt a tremor run through her.

Warwick lifted his head and for a second she thought he had mistaken it for that swift panic she had shown him in the past, then she saw he was smiling. Caressing her with lips and hands, he began slowly to undress her, prolonging it into a ritual until anticipation became a fever and her fingers dug jerkily into the muscles of his shoulders. He lowered her to the bed then, discarding his own clothes with rough haste to come down beside her, mouth at her breast and hands moving on her in sensual, experienced arousal.

His knowledge of her body's sensitivity far surpassed her own—his touch, sometimes light, sometimes abrasive and demanding, persuaded her inexorably towards the act which love and an unendurable physical need demanded. The aching hunger for his possession finally overrode all else. Eyes closed, she reached for him blindly and felt him move over her, her senses glorying in the weight and strength of his seeking body.

As his arms locked beneath her he sighed harshly and

whispered, 'God, you'll never know how I've waited for this!' then his mouth fastened on hers and he abandoned himself to the urgency of overwhelming desire.

The pressures which had seemed unbearable only a short while before, now intensified until she was beyond thought or reason. Devoured by them she twisted and strained frenziedly towards she knew not what. When at last the fluid ecstasy of release poured through her, she made a thin, high sound in her throat, dazedly conscious of Warwick holding her tightly and murmuring words she could not understand. Then the tension gradually drained from her rigid form and she returned to awareness.

Her face was pressed into Warwick's shoulder and she fought her mouth clear to gasp for breath, feeling the rapid rise and fall of his chest above her and the film of sweat on his skin. After a moment he raised himself on to his elbows and she turned her head to gaze up at him, eyes still darkened by wonder at the explosion of sensation.

He bent his head to kiss her, smiling slightly as he read her expression, and said softly, 'The French call it the little death.'

It shouldn't have been appropriate, and yet it was. For a moment she had thought the searing feeling must end in oblivion.

'Is it always like that?' she asked, still shaken.

'No.' He traced a finger down her cheek, then said, 'It takes the right combination of people.'

'Even for you?'

Hearing the doubt and uncertainty in her voice, he smiled again and said gently, 'Yes, even for me.'

Reassured, Lauren gave a fluttering sigh. Warwick kissed her again and made a move to draw away, and protestingly she held on to him.

Laughing under his breath, he said, 'Let me go. I'm crushing you.'

He was, but the discomfort was unimportant. Somehow this closeness in the aftermath of passion seemed almost as necessary as what had gone before.

'I don't mind,' she told him.

'You will tomorrow when you ache,' he said, his expression softening into tenderness. 'I'm no lightweight and you're a fragile little thing.' Maintaining the embrace, he rolled on to his side and tucked her head under his chin. Half whispering, he told her, 'And now you'll get cramp.'

She lay in a drifting lethargy, mindlessly happy until his prediction was proved and she was forced to move and free herself. She did it reluctantly, and Warwick slid an arm underneath her as she settled back.

'Wake up for a moment.'

'I am awake.'

To demonstrate she rubbed her cheek against the rough hair covering his chest, and a smile in his voice, he said, 'Don't do that. We're going to be cool and calm for a moment while you listen to me.'

'What are you going to tell me?'

The smile gone, he put his hand under her chin, tilting her face up towards him. 'That I love you. In case you didn't know, the acid test with a man comes after he's had what he wanted. You found out for yourself that some of us aren't to be trusted beforehand, but afterwards you get the truth.' He touched his lips to her shoulder, sliding them across the smooth skin. 'So I'm telling you now.'

She was silent, choked by her own feelings, and framing her face with his hands, Warwick ordered, 'Say something.'

Lauren lowered her lashes. 'I think I did.' Remembering, colour flowed up to her temples.

'Oh, yes, my darling, you did.' He laughed softly, mocking her, but without malice. 'Things even I didn't dream of when I used to watch you sitting at your office desk. But say them to me again.'

Cheeks still burning, she shook her head, and he grinned lazily and sat up to reach for his cigarettes. 'I'm going down to get my drink in a moment. Do you want one?'

'Not unless you're having coffee.'

'I'll make it for you.'

Totally unselfconscious, he got out of bed and shrugged into his robe, and caught watching him, it was Lauren who flushed. He returned with their drinks and her dressing gown, dropping it on the foot of the bed before slipping his watch from his wrist to set the alarm.

'What time does Mandy go in to you in the mornings?'

'About half past seven, usually.'

'I have to be away from here by then. I've set up another meeting with Rouillière and I shall have to go home first to pack for the trip.' His brows were drawn together as he concentrated on the fiddling task and replaced the watch in position, but the expression faded as he glanced down at her. 'So we've got until seven o'clock.'

Sitting down beside her, he drew back the quilt and ran the palm of his hand across her stomach before bringing it up and delicately enclosing the tip of her breast between finger and thumb. Immediately her body went taut and he smiled, watching her face with intent eyes as he slowly rotated his fingers.

She made no attempt to hide her reactions, and, his voice reflective, Warwick said, 'You've come a long way in a couple of hours.'

The fingers ceased their torment and gently pushed

her back. Her breath catching in her throat, Lauren gazed up at him as he leaned over her, his hands either side of her head. Softly and musingly, he said, 'I wonder how far I can take you by morning?' then he laughed.

'One way and another, my darling, you're costing me a good many sleepless nights!'

CHAPTER TEN

WARWICK woke her by rasping his chin across her shoulder, then kissing the faint red mark he had left. When she opened her eyes he said, 'Time to go back to your own nest, darling. There are stirrings in the colony.'

She said drowsily, 'Warwick . . .?' and he grinned.

'Who else would it be? But I'll cure you of calling me Warwick if it kills me!'

He slid out of bed and she watched him collect up his razor and shaving lotion, tears stinging her eyes because he was leaving.

'When will you be back?' she asked.

'I'm not sure. Probably about three days, but don't do anything or plan anything until I see you again.' His voice seemed to hold a particular meaning, but before she could examine the words he came back and kissed her, a brief, hard kiss. 'I'll ring you. Think of me.'

Back in her own room she could think of nothing else. Rachel still insisted on supervising Mandy first thing to save her from getting up early, and after Mandy had been in to kiss her good morning, Lauren lay back to lose herself again in her idyllic reverie.

It was broken when Rachel appeared, pausing in the doorway to yawn before she commented, 'I hope my sacrifice last night wasn't in vain.'

'What sacrifice?' Lauren enquired, amused but bewildered.

'I made James sit through the most boringly incomprehensible play possible. He wanted to abandon it after the first act, so I had to pretend to be enthralled.

Then when at last it was over I confessed to a yearning for lobster and begged to be taken for a meal. I had indigestion half the night, and James can't decide whether I've taken leave of my senses or I'm pregnant. He's been giving me some very odd looks this morning.'

She yawned again, and said goodhumouredly, 'So I trust you didn't waste the opportunity.' She contemplated Lauren's betraying expression with a smile. 'No, I see you didn't. I thought not when Rick wished me such a cheerful goodbye just now.'

Absently re-tying the sash of her elegant housecoat, she grinned, and on the way out added, 'Don't bother to get up for a while. Mrs Penkridge is here, so catch up on your sleep!'

When she had gone, Lauren felt her heightened colour recede to leave her face cold. It wasn't Rachel who was likely to be pregnant! She felt a clutch of jolting fright in the pit of her stomach. Last night she had been fleetingly aware of the risk, but she had swept it aside, too caught up by desire and the expression of her love for Warwick to heed it. Viewed in the cold light of day everything seemed very different. She checked dates in her mind, praying it was unlikely but knowing the reverse was true and it was all too possible. She had been determined not to marry Warwick, but she wondered if her resolve would stand up now.

He rang her from Paris that night, the warmth in his voice coming through on the crackling line, and again the next evening to say he would be flying home the following morning and the Rouillière contract was now in the hands of the lawyers. Lauren was relieved it had gone through, but her enthusiasm was tempered by preoccupation with her fear, and picking up the note in her voice, Warwick asked sharply, 'What's the matter?'

'Nothing,' she said, trying to infuse it with conviction.

He paused as though he had been about to say something and changed his mind. Finally he said, 'I'll be home tomorrow—and I love you.'

He was delayed by engine trouble, so that it was after dinner when he arrived. Lauren heard him halt by the study door to exchange some remark with James, then he came into the lounge and dumped his cases and coat on a chair. Observing his action with faint censure, Rachel invited, 'Make yourself at home,' but with his eyes fixed on Lauren, Warwick gave her only a brief smile, and she commented, 'I see. Will you want dinner?'

He shook his head. 'Not for a while anyway. I shan't feel human until I've had a shower. I'll have a brandy, though. Give it to Lauren to bring up to me.'

'Certainly,' said Rachel, in carefully impassive tones, and Warwick sent her a quick, grateful grin and bent his head to kiss Lauren as he went by.

'Give me ten minutes,' he said.

Lauren carried the brandy up when the time had elapsed, uncomfortably aware of Rachel's concealed amusement. Warwick was already dressed again, the strong black hair springing away from his face in spite of being still wet. As she put the glass down he crossed the room with quick strides and took her in his arms, resting his chin on the top of her head.

'All right,' he said, 'What is it?'

She swallowed, knowing her voice would quiver if she spoke, and Warwick said into the pause, 'Don't bother to answer—I know. You're afraid I could have got you pregnant.'

'Yes,' she whispered.

He released her and turned away to pick up the brandy. Facing her again, he said deliberately, 'I tried my level best to anyway.'

At first she thought she must somehow have

misunderstood, though the meaning of the words seemed plain enough. In stunned disbelief, she said at last, 'Say that again.'

'You heard. I may be lacking in morals by some standards, but you know my opinions on carelessness.'

'But . . . why?'

'To *make* you marry me,' he told her, his voice almost curt.

'I can't, Warwick,' she said helplessly. 'You know I can't. We could never get away with pretending I'd been married before. You're far too well known and the gossip columns would have it in no time. I'd be a social disaster for you. There's your parents and James and Rachel and the rest of your family, and all the people like Charles Tennant that you do business with. And can't you just imagine it at Fenmore's! Meg would never need anything else to talk about!' She shuddered. 'And we couldn't ever tell them the truth, because of Mandy. She'll have to learn one day that she's illegitimate, but the true facts she must never know.'

Still watching her, he nodded. 'Yes, I knew that was what you'd say. You've got this bloody insane belief that something which happened seven years ago, something in no way your fault, has made you . . .' He shrugged, 'Oh, I don't know . . . inferior . . . unfit.'

His summing up was so accurate that it left her with nothing to say, and he went on, 'So it might cause a minor sensation. It would be an ordeal for you for a while, but that's the only way it would affect me. For myself, I just don't care! If I fell on my face in business and made a fool of myself—yes, I should mind that being spread around—that's my area of pride, but this wouldn't concern me in the slightest! My parents and immediate family can be told the truth, and they're the only ones who matter. I don't give a damn what anybody else thinks!'

He pushed himself away from the dressing table and came back to her, sliding his hand under the weight of her hair to hold her neck. 'I knew the way your mind was working the other night. If we just lived together, ironically enough, people wouldn't take any notice, but I don't want a permanent mistress, and for you it would be a lifetime of embarrassment with passports and hotels and presentation lines at dinners. You're not thick-skinned enough to take it and you know it. I want us to be married.'

He kissed her with a sudden savage passion, forcing her head back against his arm, then said harshly, 'And I hope my efforts took care of any more argument!'

Lauren was silent, her face eloquent of apprehension and lingering doubt, and his fingers dug into her arms for a moment, then fell away. His lips twisting in self-disgust, he said, 'So now you know what I can be reduced to. I didn't try to argue it out with you before—you might have taken it into your head to be noble and self-sacrificing, and I didn't dare risk you disappearing on me, so with absolute, complete, utter bloody selfishness I tried to make sure of you. It wasn't until I heard your voice on the phone the other night that it occurred to me to wonder how you might feel about it. The only excuse I can offer is that I love you.'

Avoiding her gaze, he turned with a sharp movement to pick up the brandy glass again. Lauren had never seen him unsure of himself, and the rare evasiveness moved her unbearably, bringing tears which threatened to blind her. He had asked her to marry him before, told her he loved her, shown her, from little things to the way he made love to her, but she had never thought it possible until now that his feelings could in any way match her own. He had always seemed too self-sufficient, too powerful, too arrogant to need her as she needed him. There were difficulties and embarrassments to be faced—she couldn't disregard all the obstacles as easily as he did, but she could do it if it was for Warwick as well as herself.

He was little more than an outline in her blurred sight, but she smiled and said, 'Which were you hoping for, a red-haired girl or a black-haired boy?'

As he swung quickly round, she went on, 'Perhaps we ought to get married fairly soon, just in case.'

His arms closed round her so tightly she had to fight to breathe. She protested, and he eased the pressure and demanded roughly, 'How soon?'

'Give me time to buy a dress,' she said, her voice unsteady.

Warwick bent his head to kiss her, parting her lips with a hard hunger. She felt the dormant desire come to life in him, and he laughed against the side of her neck.

'I wonder if you know what you're letting yourself in for? Are you prepared to send me out each morning in a suitable state to resist the temptations of your replacement?'

With a snap Lauren said, 'I'll interview her!'

'Nothing over twenty-five,' he told her. His hands slid down her back to her hips, holding her against him. 'And I like them small and slim.' As her hands clenched into fists on his chest, he whispered, 'With long red hair and golden-brown eyes.'

'Fifty and a bun!' Lauren returned, laughing up at him. The laughter died as she recognised the silent message in his darkened eyes, and she drew in a quick, shallow breath.

He lowered his head and touched his mouth to her throat. 'I've been living on a memory for two days,' he said, his voice thickening. 'And there are parts of you I can't reach to kiss while we're standing up.'

'Rick!' she protested uncertainly. 'Rachel ... your dinner ...'

'Won't be for some time,' he murmured. 'In fact, if my sister is the intelligent, perceptive woman I've always believed her to be, I doubt if she'll even start cooking it!'